Passing Through Water

Catrina J. Sparkman

ISBN-13: 978-0692484241

ISBN-10: 0692484248

Published by:

The Ironer's Press
PO Box 1122
Madison, Wi 53701

Also by Catrina J. Sparkman

Doing Business with God: An Everyday Guide to Prayer & Journaling

Intimacy the Beginning of Authority

Intercession 101: The Heartbeat of God

Divine Revelation for a Twitter Generation

DEDICATION

This book is dedicated to every child that has ever been hurt in the house of God. For your destiny, for your soul, for your healing—

A demand

Now this is what the LORD says—

He who created you, Jacob,
He who formed you, Israel:
"Do not fear, for I have redeemed you;
I have summoned you by name; you are mine.
2 When you pass through the waters,
I will be with you;
and when you pass through the rivers,
they will not sweep over you.
When you walk through the fire,
you will not be burned;
the flames will not set you ablaze.
3 For I am the LORD your God,
the Holy One of Israel, your Savior;
I give Egypt for your ransom,
Cush and Seba in your stead.
4 Since you are precious and honored in my sight,
and because I love you,
I will give people in exchange for you,
nations in exchange for your life.

Isaiah 43: 1-4

Passing Through Water

Prologue

Baton Rouge, Louisiana, summer of 1972

Joshua Keys, African American male, toasted yellow complexion, looks to be biracial, most probably is not. Joshua was orphaned, brought to the hospital, shortly after a home delivery. His mother, a disheveled, but clearly beautiful girl of seventeen, walked into the hospital at 3:00 AM and handed the baby boy to an attendant by the name of Sara Stands. Trembling, she reached behind the nurse's counter and offered up the baby boy. "His name is Joshua, make sure you tell 'em that."

It had been Sara's day off, but she had come in at the last minute to work the night shift for a fellow staffer whose child had gotten sick. Sara had been working at that same nurse's station for over twenty years, and she was a praying woman. So she knew that it was God who had sent her there on her off day to collect the beautiful, butter colored child who looked to be not even a week old. Sara held the baby in her arms, who, she decided, had the most inquisitive eyes for a newborn she had ever seen. She said a prayer for the frightened mother as she watched her scurry out the door. Then she began to tell the infant about another great Joshua who lived a long time ago.

"They called him Joshua, son of Nun, just like you. Joshua, son of Nun grew up to do great things for God. He didn't repeat the mistakes of his guardians, just like you won't repeat the mistakes of the one who carried you. Joshua believed God, and God used Joshua to take his people into the Promised Land. That's exactly what God is going to do for you, little Joshua, son of nobody. You're going to lead His people out of darkness into a mighty light."

Sara held little Joshua close. She rocked him, fed him, prayed for him, and she spoke into his future all night long. She bound up spirits of loneliness, rejection, and self-loathing. Spirits that were bound to come looking for a baby left the way Joshua had been left. She prayed that Joshua might grow strong in the Lord--in his power, character, and might. She prayed that he would be given favor in the foster care system and find shelter in a good God-fearing home. She prayed for his career choice, his friends, his future wife, and the children that he would one day call his own. And, at the Spirit of the Lord's prompting, Sara quoted Matthew 16:19 over baby Joshua again and again. "I will give you the keys of the kingdom of heaven. Whatever you bind on earth will be bound in heaven, and whatever you loose on earth will be loosed in heaven."

At 9:00 AM the next morning, Sara Stands called social services. One week later, Joshua Keys became a ward of the state. Sara had her contact information written in his file because she knew that a baby with such inquisitive eyes would one day come looking for information regarding his birth. And she was absolutely right, he did.

August 2005

CHAPTER 1

Houston, Texas, Monday, August 22, 2005

Joshua looked up from his position at the head of the conference table to see his secretary, Selena, strolling towards him. Selena's long caramel legs glided past the representative from the tennis shoe corporation, in the middle of his pitch, and other executives seated around the table. As she leaned down and whispered to Joshua, her loose brown hair formed a pool on the table in front of him, a private screen shielding her face and his alone.

"A Mr. Mattingham is here to see you. No appointment. I tried to tell him you were unavailable, but he insisted I tell you that the eagle has landed in New Orleans. He insisted that I tell you this immediately. Shall I call security?"

"No, have Mr. Mattingham wait for me inside my office. I'll be right there," Joshua said.

Selena slipped out of the conference room just as quietly as she had entered and closed the door behind her. Joshua waited for a pause in the rep's presentation before he stood up from the table.

"Sorry, gentlemen, but another matter has come up, and I must take my leave."

Joshua looked down to the other end of the table to his brother, and business partner, Michael Dutton. Mike and Joshua exchanged a slight nod as Joshua headed for the door.

The rep's face flushed deep red. "Mr. Keys, please. If you would only give us a moment more of your time. I can show you the market projection for our fall line."

"Not necessary. I like what I've seen so far. I especially like that your shoes are American made. I wouldn't want anyone using my name to break child labor laws or to promote sweatshops overseas."

"Our company is morally sound. I think you'll find our policies and practices to be in keeping with your more recently publicized Christian beliefs. It's because of our common core values that our designers felt you would be the ideal face for *In Step Shoes*."

"Good. Then it looks like we have a deal. Mr. Dutton has full authority to negotiate on my behalf." Joshua exited the meeting room and walked down the long corridor that led to his private office. He knew exactly what Mattingham's cryptic message meant. It meant he had found them, his wife and son living in New Orleans. When Joshua walked through the main doors, he found the investigator waiting in the lounge area, seated on one of the sleek leather couches, perusing a copy of *Sport's Illustrated.* Joshua presumed that this was Mattingham's feeble attempt to blend in.

As a private investigator, Mattingham was a walking stereotype minus the trench coat and ridiculous hat. This was exactly the kind of seedy character you'd meet in a back alley after midnight, or in a fortune 500 company's parking structure, long after the cleaning crew had gone home. It was a small wonder that Bella, always very perceptive, hadn't seen this man coming a mile off.

"He preferred to wait for you in the lobby," Selena said, as if she were reading Joshua's thoughts. Joshua could tell by his secretary's questioning glances that she wanted to know what business this man could possibly have with him. It wasn't company related, and Joshua saw no need to offer any explanations concerning his personal affairs. What he did do was ask her to hold his calls as he led Mattingham into his office.

CHAPTER 2

Mattingham walked into Joshua's office and let out a low appreciative whistle. "I was under the impression that anonymity was paramount in your profession," Joshua said.

"What's that?"

"I asked my secretary to have you wait inside my office, you declined."

Mattingham shrugged. "She seemed a bit jittery about my being here. I thought it would be best for me to wait out in the open. Sometimes keeping things out in the open makes people less suspicious. If ya know what I mean."

"You found them."

Mattingham handed Joshua a large envelope. "Goes by the name, Rosemary LeBlanc. The kid, she calls Matthew. Pretty much works every day. For the most part, don't talk to nobody, kind of keeps to herself. She's got this cart in the French Quarter, on Bourbon Street."

Mattingham studied Joshua carefully as he flipped through the photos. This guy was cool. Real cool. No hint of emotion ever crossed his face, and he didn't allow his eyes to linger on the pictures of his estranged wife for more than a second. Even though she was quite the looker, smooth butterscotch skin, big brown eyes, that wild curly mane, and for a woman who'd given birth, Mattingham had to admit, she had a great body too. Standing next to the famous, former NBA superstar, Mattingham could see that the two of them were almost an exact pair. They could easily pass for brother and sister. At the very least, black Barbie and Ken dolls. He was beginning to understand why a man of Joshua's means, would spend the small fortune that he had to find her.

Mattingham watched as Joshua ran his fingers slowly over the image of the kid she called Matthew playing basketball on the playground with a group of older kids. First time he'd laid eyes on the boy in five years. "Kid's got a jumper like his old man, eh?"

"Tell me about this cart. What does she sell?"

"She makes jewelry for a living. Some of it's pretty decent. She's down there every day, Monday through Saturday. Sundays she usually stays home, plays games, and reads to the kid."

"She can't possibly be making enough to live on doing that," Joshua said flipping through the rest of the photos.

"She seems to eek out a decent enough living. Looks like she may have something going on with the landlord. Rent is, apparently, on the house. "

The look of anger that flashed across Joshua's face nearly scared the crap out of Mattingham. They didn't call this guy, Bad Boy Joshua Keys, for nothing. The ex-ball player's temper was legendary, and Mattingham did not want to be on the receiving end of his wrath. He figured wifey ran away because Joshua was beating the stew out of her. But, hey, that wasn't his business or his problem. His job was simply to find them, not to get involved in his clients' "domesticated" affairs. Mattingham reached into his bag slowly and pulled out another envelope. He was careful, not to make any sudden moves with this one. The PI chose his next words carefully. "I have more sensitive pictures if ya need 'em. For uh, you know . . . legal purposes. I find that the courts don't take too kindly to wives who've been caught in the act."

"I told you, my main purpose in hiring you was to find my son. As far as his mother is concerned, she's a free agent. She can do as she pleases." Joshua motioned for the pictures. "Are these the masters?"

Mattingham reached into his briefcase and pulled out a disc and handed it to Joshua.

"You don't have any other pictures of my wife floating around, do you?" His face remained placid, but the threat in the ex-ball player's voice was clear.

"You mean like on the Internet? That would be a breach of our contractual agreement, and for that you could sue the socks off of me. I don't want to be sued, Mr. Key's." *Or have the crap beat out of me either.*

Joshua walked over to his desk, opened a large ledger and wrote Mattingham a check. "Serve her the papers, and buy something."

Mattingham's eyes bucked when he saw the check. "This isn't the jewelry counter at *Tiffany's,* Mr. Keys. What do you expect me to buy?"

"First, take $1000 dollars of that money and buy yourself a decent suit. I need you to pretend to be a businessman who wants to have an expensive piece made for his wife. You'll have to arrange a chance meeting before you serve her the papers, to commission something. I don't care what you buy. Just make sure you pay her well enough so she and my son are not living like paupers, until these court proceedings are handled. Consider the suit a gift from me, and we'll call another ten percent, $2500, an administrative fee, for your time. The rest I expect you to put in my wife's hand. Understand?"

"Sure, but—"

Joshua held out his hand to Mattingham, who read the gesture loud and clear. Rich people speak for, this meeting is over. I don't ever wanna see your stinkin' face again. *That's fine by me, buddy. Just fine.*

Mattingham fixed a smile in place and shook Joshua's outstretched hand. "Very nice doing business with you, Mr. Keys. I'll be sure to send that package to you by carrier mail right away."

❧

Joshua pulled a handkerchief from his breast pocket, and wiped away the remaining moisture from Mattingham's plump, sweaty hand. As he did, he tried to shake the thought that he'd just made a deal with the devil. He walked over to the large leather sectional that flanked the fireplace in his office and took a seat on the couch. He picked up the second envelope Mattingham had left for him, opened it, and studied the pictures of his wife in bed with another man.

Joshua could feel his body heat skyrocketing. He closed his eyes, tucked his head between his legs, and took deep, cleansing breaths, as he tried to clear the images from his mind. When that brought him no relief, Joshua lowered his body down onto the floor, into a kneeling position.

"I'm a need a little help down here. I don't think I have the strength to do what you're asking." Twenty minutes later, Joshua arose and lit the fireplace. He took the second batch of photos, and the disc Mattingham had left with him and threw them into the fire.

CHAPTER 3

New Orleans, Louisiana, Thursday, Aug. 24, 2005

Bella dropped the coins in the open palm of the man's hand, a math teacher from a nearby middle school. "You have a great day, Mr. Moore. Thank you for supporting *Rosemary's Creations.*" Because of the order of friendship bracelets he'd placed last week, Bella could now afford to pay her booth fees for the day. She'd also be able to give Jabari lunch money for his field trip tomorrow. Now, if Mrs. Cartwright would only show, she'd have the money she needed to make her rent this month as well.

"Please, call me, Tyler." the math teacher said in a voice that told Bella he admired much more than her bracelets. "So far your bracelets have been the only effective way I've come up with to get the kids to pay attention in class. If these bracelets are the hit I expect them to be with my sixth period, I'm sure you'll be seeing much more of me."

His hand lingered in Bella's just a minute too long, before she pumped it in a business-like handshake and sent him on his way. Sometimes she felt like she had a sign on her forehead that advertised her former life. A sign that said, 'still open for business.' And, yes, she told herself, despite what she had to do last month to make ends meet, it was still her former life.

Bella scanned the busy street dotted with merchants hocking their wares, musicians peddling their blues, panhandlers, clowns, and mimes looking for signs of Mrs. Cartwright. Everybody had a hustle on Bourbon Street. Nothing was too ridiculous or over the top. Bella felt her stomach tighten as the hour grew later. Rent was due three days ago, and like a fool, she had used her rent money to buy the stone needed for Mrs. Cartwright's necklace. A customer had burned Bella on an expensive custom piece once before. She could just kick herself for not making Mrs. Cartwright pay a deposit.

The last thing in the world she needed, or wanted, was to have to report back to Charlie Terry empty handed. Bile rose up in her throat at the thought of having to make alternative arrangements.

She and Jabari had been evicted once, five years ago, when Bella first moved back to New Orleans. Jabari, who had tried to be brave, had come home to find their things outside on the curb. Bella saw the worry in his six-year-old face, and heard the fear in his voice when he asked her if they were going to have to live outdoors like the people they saw pushing shopping carts up and down the street. In that moment, Bella decided that she would never be evicted again. She would do whatever she had to do to keep a roof over her son's head.

They drove around the city all night, until she found a vacancy in the Dunbar Street apartment complex located in an older section of town known as the Lower Ninth Ward.

It wasn't much, certainly couldn't compare to where her child had spent the first six years of his life, but it was all they could afford, and for the last five years it had been home . . . *well not home*. Bella corrected herself. Home, for Jabari, would always be wherever Joshua was. What they had here was a roof that kept out the rain.

A Creole woman with red hair and green eyes approached Bella's booth and picked up a jade necklace and bracelet set. Bella quickly set her thoughts aside and angled the mirror towards the woman.

"That jade really picks up the color in your eyes," Bella said.

The woman said nothing, but smiled her approval, and a few minutes later asked if Bella had earrings to match.

Bella counted the profit in her drawer. Thanks to the Creole woman, she had one hundred and fifty dollars—after booth fees and Jabari's field trip money. One hundred fifty dollars wouldn't pay the rent, but if she was careful in her spending this week, they could at least eat. There was only thirty minutes left before the vendors had to be packed up and off the street and Mrs. Cartwright was still a no show.

Every week the blue haired woman visited Bella's booth, looking and looking but never buying, even though she had plenty money to burn. The rumor on Bourbon Street was that Mrs. Cartwright was crazy rich. Merchants, and shop owners throughout the Quarter, referred to the days that Mrs. Cartwright came to shop as Black Fridays. A business that had been operating in the red all week could turn a profit from just one of Mrs. Cartwright's buys. All the vendors catered to Mrs. Cartwright like she was royalty.

Personally, Bella thought the woman was the poster child for over accessorizing. She wore a ring on every finger and often more than one necklace at a time. This wasn't costume jewelry either, Bella knew her stones. Mrs. Cartwright wore the real thing. Her driver, a tall, stately, kind-eyed black fellow in his late fifties, followed Mrs. Cartwright wordlessly to shop after shop like a pack animal, laden down with her purchases. Every Friday she breezed in and out of the expensive shops and boutiques shopping indiscriminately—that is, until she got to Bella's cart. Then the woman would pick through her things methodically, scrutinizing the color and hue of every stone, while Bella watched on like a starving puppy, waiting for Mrs. Cartwright to throw her a bone. After weeks of this routine, Bella realized that Mrs. Cartwright probably would never buy anything from her. So when Mrs. Cartwright came sniffing around her booth, two weeks ago, Bella ignored her. She busied herself counting inventory and straightening her jewelry racks. Mrs. Cartwright pulled out a magazine with a dog-eared page and dropped it down in front of Bella.

"Can you make me a necklace that looks exactly like this one?" Bella stared at the picture of the triple strand freshwater pearl necklace, with the large teardrop sapphire at the center. The sapphire pictured was of first rate quality. The bluest blue Bella had ever seen.

"Well . . . the pearls for sure, that wouldn't be a problem. I could get a sapphire for you, Mrs. Cartwright, but I'm afraid it wouldn't be anywhere near the quality of the one shown in this picture. This necklace looks very expensive."

"I had my jeweler check into it for me, $225,000. There only one like it in the whole world. I don't want to pay a nickel over $1200. Can you make it for me?"

Bella's jaw nearly dropped to the ground. But she quickly collected herself. She nodded her head in the affirmative and told Mrs. Cartwright the necklace would be ready in two weeks.

Bella heard the clip clop of shoes against the cobblestone pavement. She looked up to see the driver, as usual, loaded down with Mrs. Cartwright's things. "Oh, Rosemary, I'm so glad I made it. I've been dying to see my necklace all week. I hope you have it."

"Of course, Mrs. Cartwright, I have it right here." Bella pulled the sapphire necklace out of one of the velvet bags she saved for her customers who made the most expensive purchases. She had to admit, it was the most exquisite piece she'd ever created. She could never afford to wear anything like it. Mrs. Cartwright fished through her purse until she found her glasses.

"Ah, lovely," the older woman breathed. Mrs. Cartwright opened her purse again, this time pulling out the dog-eared magazine page. She held the necklace up to the picture on the page.

"Almost a perfect match don't you think?" Bella said.

Mrs. Cartwright frowned. "Oh dear, I'm afraid it's not the same."

"What do you mean?" Bella said, fighting to keep her voice even.

"The stone, it's simply not the same. Look, this one is cerulean, yours looks well . . . navy. What on earth is special about a navy sapphire? I simply can't be caught dead in this thing! You'll have to redo it."

"Mrs. Cartwright, the stone is non- refundable. I can't take it back!"

"Well you certainly can't expect me to pay for it. It's not what I ordered." And before Bella could respond Mrs. Cartwright stalked off.

The driver hesitated for a moment, his kind eyes making contact with Bella's. He was giving her the look—that universal look that poor folks give each other, when rich folks say or do something utterly clueless. His look said to Bella, *I know what you're going through sista, keep your head up.* It took everything inside of Bella to keep from crying.

Don't worry you can always work something out with Terry. The mere thought of it made her absolutely sick. The bile in her belly rose quickly, too quickly for Bella to tamp it back down. Before she knew it, she was releasing her insides into a bank of nearby bushes. Hot tears burned against her lids. *Why didn't I insist on a six hundred dollar deposit? How could I be so stupid?* Bella slowly began packing up her cart. Maybe there was another way. Maybe she could get out of this jam with her body and spirit intact.

Bella reached for the cheap gold chain around her neck and fingered the hand engraved diamond encrusted platinum wedding band she kept out of sight, tucked safely beneath her clothing, next to her heart. She thought for the millionth time about hocking it. Life would be so much easier if she did, but like every other time she'd been in financial crisis she abandoned the thought. This ring, with its four words engraved on the inside: *For Bella my heart*, was the only symbol of hope Bella had left. It was hope that she could get her life together on her own terms. Hope that she would one day have lasting change. And hope that when her change did come, she would be the one to go back and find him this time. She would be able to look at him when that happened and say with complete honesty, *I've been desperate enough to sell my soul, but never so desperate that I would sell your heart.*

Hocking the ring was not an option, but Bella did have a lunch date scheduled with her mother that afternoon. Maybe she could convince Sylvia to give her the money, just a small loan, one her father would never have to know about.

Bella's father was the pastor of a very prominent church in New Orleans and her parents were, by no means, hurting for money. She knew her mother would spend three times what Bella was asking for on whatever outfit she'd wear to lunch that day. And she might, for once, be in a generous mood. Generous enough to not see her only child and grandchild tossed out into the streets. Bella straightened her back a little, and although her heart was heavy, she tried to hold her head up. This was not going to defeat her. If appealing to her mother didn't work, she would just have to try dodging Terry for a couple of more days, and come out to sell on a Sunday. Bella had gotten pretty good at dodging bill collectors. Heck, she'd been dodging the repo man now for the last month.

Bella's custom was to reserve Sunday as a day of rest for her and Jabari. For some reason, she'd held onto to that no-working-on-Sunday rule, even though they weren't big on going to church these days. A throwback from her days growing up as a PK (preacher's kid) she guessed. Nowadays, Bella and

Jabari were more like bedside Baptists, but if things didn't work out with her mother, she would have no other choice but to come out on Sunday, and hope that the Sunday crowd would be in a buying mood. And as for Jesus and the Sabbath . . . well . . . He could just add that to her already incredibly long list of sins, cause a girl's gotta do, what a girl's gotta do. The only thing that was certain for Bella was that she could not run. Not this time. She could never do that to Jabari again.

"Excuse me, ma'am."

Bella looked in the direction of the voice. A squat balding white man, with squirrelly eyes, and a raspy voice was leaning up against a tree.

"I see that you're packing up for the day, but do you think you'd have time for one more sell? I'd make it worth your while." Immediately, Bella's antennae went up, and she found herself disliking this man, but he wore an expensive looking suit and a smile, so Bella put on her best customer-friendly voice. "What can I do for you, sir?"

"I overheard the unfortunate exchange you were having with the lady a few minutes ago. Some people, you can never please them. They don't know quality when they see it. I'm a business man. I like to collect beautiful things on my travels, you know, for my wife. I'd like to take that necklace off your hands."

Well, I'll be, thought, Bella. *You really are real, and you care for me. Sorry, for all the times I ever doubted you.*

"My wife loves blue," the man continued. "How much is the necklace?"

"It's $1200, sir."

He whistled. "That's pretty steep for an outdoor market."

"Do you know anything about jewelry?"

"A bit."

"For the quality and cut of the stone, it's quite reasonable. In fact it's underpriced."

"Yeah, but you can't return the stone, right? I mean that's what I heard you tell the old bag."

"It's a final sale item," Bella said quietly.

"I'll tell you what, I'm feeling generous today. Why don't I take it off your hands for say, 350?"

"Sir, the stone alone cost twice that much."

The man shrugged. "What do you care? Just write it off as a business loss. That's the cost of doing business right? We've all had to eat it every now and again, on a few bad deals."

Bella's heart dropped, but she took the $350 cash, and wrapped the necklace up for the man. "I really appreciate this." He took his purchase and turned to leave.

"My wife loves blue. Hey, you know, I think I've seen you someplace before. I can't think of where, but I know I've seen you."

"Well, I'm here every day. Monday through Saturday," Bella said, no longer caring to hide her annoyance at this point.

"No, that's not it. I know I've seen you someplace else." He snapped his fingers. "Hey, I know, *Sports Illustrated June 2000.* You're Bad Boy Joshua Key's wife, right? The wife and I are huge fans. Huge! That's you right? I mean your hair is a little different but that's you, right?"

"Yeah, that's me."

"Wait till I tell my wife, she's never gonna believe this. Mind if I take a picture?"

Bella hid her face with her hand and backed away. "No. No pictures."

"Okay sure, sure, I understand. Just one more thing." The man produced a legal size envelope out of his breast pocket and handed it to Bella. "You've been served."

Before Bella could respond or react the man was already gone. Bella's hands trembled as she stared down at the envelope. She didn't have to read its contents to know that Joshua had found her.

CHAPTER 4

Bella sat in her car and wept bitterly. The tears rolled down her face and smeared the ink on the court documents. This wasn't supposed to happen. Not yet, and certainly not like this. She had found out the hard way that Joshua could track her whereabouts with her credit card purchases, so this last time she'd bought two one way tickets to New York on the credit card. From New York, she paid cash and she and Jabari had hopped a train back to the one place Bella had sworn she'd never return. She changed their names, even managed to get them new social security numbers. She figured that Louisiana would be the last place in the world that he would come looking for her.

Joshua had filed for legal separation on the grounds of desertion, and now according to the papers, he wanted a divorce and joint custody of Jabari. She knew that she should be grateful that considering everything that had happened between them, he still wanted Jabari. But that wasn't enough. He had always wanted Jabari. She had left in the first place because loving Jabari and tolerating her was never enough. Bella laid her head against the steering wheel. "You know I can't afford to run. So what do you suggest I do?"

But like all the other times she had tried to petition God, Bella heard nothing. The scripture verse her mother always quoted to her as a child ran back and forth like background music in her head. *The way of the transgressor is hard. The way of the transgressor is hard.*

Bella sighed. She should have known better than to try and seek council from Him on anything. He never did anything for her, certainly never protected her. Bella took a compact out of her purse and began to apply a fresh coat of make-up to her face. She exhaled deeply, put her key in the ignition, and pointed the car in the direction of Lucchini's, the Italian restaurant where she'd agreed to meet her mother.

CHAPTER 5

Bella entered the restaurant and greeted her mother with an air-kiss. Always the proper pastor's wife, Sylvia was decked out in classic First Lady style. She wore a purple three-piece St. Johns suit, a string of pearls, a large Sunday-go-to-meeting hat, gloves, and matching purse.

"Bella Rose, have you been crying?"

"I'm fine, Mama."

"Well you don't look it. Your cheeks are absolutely flushed."

"Excuse me, Mama."

Bella ran into the bathroom. Moments later she found herself dry heaving into the toilet until she couldn't heave anymore. When Bella came out of the stall her mother was waiting for her with a wet paper towel in her hand and a look of concern etched across her face.

"Whatever it is, Bella Rose, I want you to know, you can always tell your mama, always." It was moments like these when Bella saw something in her mother's eyes other than judgment, something akin to real care and kindness, that made her want to crawl up in her lap and cry. *If I had told you when I was little, would you have believed me?* Tears rolled down Bella's face.

"What is it, baby?"

And because Bella couldn't tell her the real thing, that thing that had been wrong for the last twenty years, she said the thing that was lying right there on the surface. "I spent money I didn't have on a piece for this rich lady, and at the last minute she decided she didn't want it. I can't pay my rent."

Sylvia pulled her daughter close, and Bella held on for dear life.

"Oh, baby, I'm so sorry. Now what you should have done is get half the money up front. But never mind all of that, you stay in business long enough, you'll learn." Sylvia held Bella at arm's length and looked directly into her eyes. "Some lessons are taught, Bella Rose, and then there are those lessons that are bought."

"Yeah, I know."

"If you plan on being in business for yourself, you have to be tough. You have to learn how to thank God for those bought lessons, and keep your chin up. I bought quite a few lessons myself when your daddy was just starting out. I was the church secretary back then, you know. I had to pay all the bills. Traveling ministers would call and ask if they could rent our building to hold their revivals. Lord knows, back in those days, we could barely keep the lights on in that little storefront ourselves, so if someone was willing to pay to rent the space we sure would let them. Child, I can't tell you how many times they told us they were going to pay us after the offering. We were burned so many times by the people of God, I learned how to tell them that we were doing the work of the Lord too, and that from now on, if they rented our church, I had to see half the money up front. I learned that the hard way."

Sylvia dabbed Bella's face. "Now, don't you worry about any of this right now. We are about to have a fabulous lunch today and wonderful conversation. God always makes a way, Bella Rose, you just remember that."

Sylvia steered Bella out of the bathroom and back to their table. Just as they were arriving, a waiter appeared and set two piping hot plates down on the table in front of them.

"Thank you, Jerry."

"You're most welcome, Mrs. LeBlanc."

Bella stared at her mother questioningly.

"You were late, again, Bella Rose, so I ordered. I'd hoped you'd like my selection. But if you don't, you may choose something else."

Bella hid her growing annoyance behind a thin smile. "No Mama, the meal you've chosen for me is just fine."

"Good girl, always be open to trying new things."

Sylvia reached across the table, grabbed Bella's hand, and began to bless the food. And after she finished, Sylvia launched into a detailed description of every Sunday message her father had preached since the last time she and Bella had seen each other. This was the part about having lunch with her mother that Bella hated. The food was sure to be spectacular, but having to hear every detail about the one person, and the one place that had caused her so much pain, some days it just wasn't worth it. She imagined that her mother felt that this was her Christian duty, now that her daughter was a backslider. Bella's stomach growled as she took in the heavenly aroma of the food in front of her, but she made a meal of her water instead. Jabari loved this restaurant, and she had already determined to save the food for his supper.

"What's the matter? Don't you like the pasta?" Sylvia asked.

"It's fine. I'm just not that hungry. I think I'm going to get a doggie bag and save it for later."

Sylvia signaled the waiter, who was at their table in an instant. "Jerry, I'd like to order another plate of this to go, for my grandson, please. It's his favorite dish. Also, add an order of the seafood shrimp pasta to that order, as well. It's my daughter's favorite."

"Right away, ma'am."

Sylvia smiled ruefully at her daughter. "You can't fool me, Bella, don't forget I raised you. Eat."

Throughout lunch Bella listened to her mother chatter non-stop, jumping from one subject to the next. Bella offered an, "oh really" here and there in the conversation whenever she felt like one was required, but the whole time she was thinking of a way to ask her mother for money. Sylvia had switched gears again, for the umpteenth time. Now she was talking about the tropical storm the newscasters had predicted was heading towards New Orleans. The storm called Katrina.

"They're on the TV everyday scaring the living daylights out of people, telling the folks they oughta leave. We even know some pastors telling their congregations to leave. When I was coming up, you think we would have packed up and fled the city cause of a tiny little thing like a storm? I don't know what's gotten into these people. But you know what Pastor says."

"No, what's that?"

That was another thing that Bella hated about her mother. The way she always referred to her father as Pastor. Of course, the Right Reverend could do no wrong in the eyes of his wife. But did she have to talk about him like he was the fourth member of the godhead? Father, Son, Holy Ghost, and Pastor.

"Pastor says, the people leave 'cause they don't have any faith. Most of the ones going aren't New Orleans bred, so I can't rightly blame them. They don't know a thing about weathering through a storm."

"Mama, a man came to my booth and served me papers today. Joshua wants a divorce."

Sylvia's fork stopped mid-air.

"He wants joint custody of Jabari. He's willing to pay alimony and child support as long as he gets the right to see his son."

"Oh, baby, I'm so sorry. I really am. Here I am going on and on about the weather and you're in the middle of a major crisis. What in the world are you going to do?"

"I guess I'm going to show up to court tomorrow at 10 AM. It's an emergency hearing. The papers say I have to."

"Well you have to fight this. You can't let that awful man get custody of Jabari. Do you have an attorney? What in the world am I thinking? Of course you don't have an attorney, you can barely keep a roof over your heads."

"Mama, please. Calm down. We'll be fine. Okay?"

"Bella, if you would just come home, at least come back to the church. Your father would see that you were making steps in the right direction, and he would help you."

"Mama, please, let's not go down that road again. You know I can't do that."

"I hate this. Lord knows I hate this. How that man was able to come into our lives and turn you against your very own flesh. He fooled us all, Bella Rose. Every last one of us—even your daddy, taking him under his wing like a son. But, baby, listen to me, we are your parents, we will love you forever. My, God, Bella Rose, if you would just repent. Just say those horrible things—say that they never happened. Your daddy would forgive you, God would forgive you too. Just repent Bella and come home. We'll get the best lawyers this town has to offer, and we will fight this mess. I promise you."

"Mama, if you really want to help me and Jabari, you can help us by giving me some money on my rent just until—"

Sylvia held up her hand to silence her. "No. Now you know I can't in good consciousness give you money. I love you. You and Jabari both. I had four babies all die in my womb; you are my only living child. And from the looks of things, Jarbari's the only grandchild I'll ever have, too. But the reason you're going through what you're going through right now, with your living situation, is 'cause you need to get right with Jesus. I keep telling you, Bella Rose, that the way of the transgressor is hard."

"I know you do, Mama, but, if you could just find it in your heart to help us this one time, I won't ever ask you for anything again."

"You're a very resourceful girl. I'm sure you'll figure a way out of this."

"You'd say no, even if it means we'd be turned out onto the street? Mama, I don't have anybody else to turn to. We have no place to go."

"Nonsense, stop being so melodramatic. You can always come home."

"I can never go back there."

"I will never understand you. This is a mortal sin what you are doing, keeping your daddy from his one and only grandson. But you always where a hard-headed child."

Sylvia's words were like daggers cutting into Bella's flesh. But she held her resolve. She would not cry.

"You've left your father, left the church, everything and everybody that ever cared anything at all about you. What are you gonna do, Bella Rose, let that man take your son away from you, too? Then what will you have? Nothing at all."

"Josh wouldn't do that, Mama. He just wants to have a relationship with his son."

"According to you, he's not even Jabari's real daddy."

Bella winced at the caviler way her mother threw out this painful information from her past. The effortlessness in which it rolled off her tongue made Bella regret telling her mother something so personal and intimate.

"You'd send your boy to a man who's not even his father. God forbid, what if he did something to Jabari? The smartest thing you ever did was run away from that man."

Bella felt an old familiar rage building up on the inside. But she kept her cool and answered her mother quietly.

"Mama, Joshua legally adopted Jabari the day he was born. He is his father. He's the only father Jabari has ever known. He's never hit me or physically harmed me in any way, and he would never, ever, do anything to hurt Jabari."

"Don't you tell me what Mr. Bad Boy Joshua Keys wouldn't do. He attacked your father in the house of God." Sylvia hissed.

"Because he raped me."

"I am not— I am not going to do this with you today."

"That's right, Mama. In the house of God—"

"I won't sit here and listen to you blaspheme God's anointed."

"Over, and over again until I was fourteen years old and I had enough."

"You know what your problem is? You blame everybody else for the decisions you make. None of this foolishness ever came out before. I think you came up with this cockamamie story about your father molesting you, to justify Joshua hitting your daddy. You don't have to protect him from me, Bella Rose. There's nobody here but the two of us. For once in your life, why don't you tell the truth. Why would you run away like you did, living under assumed names like you do, if Joshua wasn't violent? And Jabari calling himself Matthew in public, you telling people your name is Rosemary. What do you think that's doing to your child's mind?"

Bella knew that part of what her mother was saying right now was true. Still, she wasn't about to own any of it, not today. Today she would lay it all down at the feet of her mother.

"Oh, you mean like the way you're always protecting Daddy? What do you think that's done to my mind all these years? Nobody's here, but you and me, Mama. So go ahead tell the truth. You had to have known."

"Jerry, Check! I am sick to death of you and all your lies. Your father never did anything but love you. I never did anything but love you. And as for these hideous allegations—my Bible tells me not to entertain accusations against an elder unless they come from two or three witnesses."

"If that god you preach about is real, then my daddy gon burn. Cause I know it happened, he know it happened, and God does too." Bella held three fingers up in the air. "See Mama, one, two, three."

In the same ceremonious fashion, Sylvia opened her wallet, and dropped one, two, three, hundred dollar bills onto the table for the waiter. She grabbed her purse, and stormed out of the restaurant. Little did they know, it would be the last time they saw each other on this side of Glory.

CHAPTER 6

New Orleans, Friday, August 25, 2005, 7AM

Bella pulled the bacon out of the oven and opened the blinds over the sink to let a little sunlight into the cramped space. When they'd first moved into the tiny apartment, Bella had wanted to paint the walls a bright sunny yellow in an attempt to bring a little cheer into the sad, depressing place. After the fifth coat, Bella realized the walls were drinking the paint, and the closest thing she ever got to the beautiful sunny color she intended was dull, muted beige. Jabari came out of the bedroom with his book bag slung over one arm and his basketball in the other. He plopped down in the chair at the kitchen table and commenced to devouring the plate of food in front of him. When he came up for air, he surveyed the suit and pumps Bella wore. "You going to the market dressed like that?"

"No market today. I have business downtown."

"What kind of business?"

Bella rubbed his head playfully. "Grown folks business."

"We not being evicted again are we?"

"I told you, I won't ever let that happen again." And because he still didn't seem convinced, and Bella didn't want her child worrying about having a roof over his head, she decided to tell him about Joshua. "I'm going to tell you something, but I want you to try not to get too excited."

"I'm chill, ma, what's up?"

"I got a letter yesterday from your father's attorney."

Jabari nearly jumped three feet into the air.
"Oh man, daddy found us! What did it say? He wants us to come home doesn't he? I knew it! I knew it!"

"Shhh, Jabari, keep your voice down. You know the walls are paper thin around here. He wants to see you. That's why I'm going to court today. We need to work out the details."

"Dad's here in New Orleans?"

"I don't know that for sure. All I know is I'm supposed to report to court today so we can work out a visitation schedule."

"Then I'm going with you."

"You have school today. Remember the field trip to the aquarium? The one you've been looking forward to all week." Jabari shook his head.

"I don't care about some stupid field trip. If my father's here, I want to see him."

A pang of bitterness hit Bella. She had been busting her butt all week to pay for that 'stupid' field trip, and to make sure he had the extra money to buy a lunch while he was there, because even if he did qualify for free lunch at school, he certainly couldn't use his free lunch voucher at the pizza parlor his teacher was taking the class to afterwards.

"I'm sure Joshua wants to see you as much as you want to see him. Maybe, we can work something out. Okay?"

"You think he'll be here today, when I get home?"

"I don't know, Jabari. We'll see. Okay?"

"Man, Dad's in Louisiana. I can't even believe it! How do you think he found us?"

Bella tore off a piece of dry toast and stuffed it into her mouth. The only thing this morning that seemed to want to stay down. "Must have hired a private eye I guess."

"You gotta admit, Ma, that's pretty cool. Wait till I tell Marcus."

"Hey, no! You don't go telling nobody about this. Our business is our business. Remember?"

Bella studied her son. He shifted his weight uncomfortably and stared down at his feet.

"Jabari, you haven't told any of the kids at school who your daddy is, have you? Well, have you?"

"Ma, chill. I didn't tell nobody. Nobody but, Marcus, and he didn't believe me no way."

Marcus was the star basketball player at the local high school and a resident in their building. Marcus and the other boys tolerated Jabari because, according to Jabari, he had game. Bella had reservations about her son hanging with the older kids, but he missed Joshua so much, and basketball seem to fill up the gaping hole left in his life she didn't have the heart to forbid it.

"You better get going, you don't want to miss your bus."

Jabari grabbed the last piece of bacon, scooped up his backpack, and his basketball—which was like a third appendage these days, and kissed Bella on the cheek before running out the door. Bella grabbed her purse. She figured with Jabari making so much noise going out the front door, she could sneak out the back. She had parked her Honda three blocks away, to avoid both the repo man and her landlord. Bella took off her high heels, closed the apartment door, and slipped out the back way. She smelled Charlie Terry's rank cigar before she bumped into him. The smell made the dry toast she'd just eaten threaten to come back up.

"Hello, Rosemary. You look awful nice today. Where you sneaking off to so early?"

"I got jury duty, Terry. You know, Uncle Sam. He says I got to be there early."

"Well I need my money. I'm not running a charity ward around here. I got bills, too."

"I'll settle up with you this evening."

"If you can't make your rent, same deal as before applies." He ran his hard calloused fingers up her arm. "I take all forms of payment. Cash, check, MasterCard, Visa . . . trim."

Bella snatched her arm away from him. "I'll have your money when I get home tonight, Terry. Cash."

Chapter 7

Houston, Friday, August 25, 2005, 9AM

After being forwarded to Joshua's secretary's voice mail for the umpteenth time, Mike leaned back in his office chair and stuck his head out the door. "Hey, I thought you said my brother was in."

"Hay is for horses, Mr. Dutton," his secretary said. Her eyes never moved from the document in front of her, and her keystroke never broke stride. "And I saw, Pastor Josh— I mean, Mr. Keys, headed towards the company chapel when I was getting off the elevator this morning."

"Thank you for self-correcting, Mrs. Berry."

"That's Mother Berry to you, young man. Mr. Keys may not want to be called Pastor Josh while he's at work, but I am always, wherever I go, a Mother in Zion."

Mike walked into the outer office and took a seat on the edge of the older woman's desk. "Very well, thank you for self-correcting, Mother Berry. But could you please stop referring to it as the company chapel, it's a mediation and reflection room. Lots of companies have them. So stop trying to make it sound—"

"Radical? I'm afraid that's what the two of you boys are."

"No, see that's exactly what we are not."

"You just keep telling yourself that, Michael, and maybe one day it'll be true."

"It is true. Progressive companies all over the world have spaces like these. Not just Home Court Advantage. And for purely economic reasons I might add. Reflection spaces allow employees to relax. When employees are relaxed, they're naturally more creative. Increased creativity means increased productivity, which translates into increased profit margins, which means company heads, such as myself, can afford to pay better wages. And here's the best part about it, Mother Berry. Relaxed, well paid people don't come to work and shoot up the place."

"Well in that case I say thank you, Jesus, for the company chapel. Still, from now on, I think I'm going to carry a little blessed oil in my purse. Won't hurt to anoint the doorpost in the morning before the rest of the staff gets here." Mike chuckled and rose from the desk.

"Whatever makes you happy. Lord knows, I don't want you coming up in here toting no pistol either. I'm gon head over to Key Town for a bit. If anybody asks."

"Don't forget about your 11:00."

Mike snapped his fingers. "Already did. Who am I meeting with?"

"Ad executives from that tennis shoe company. I'll send the information to your Blackberry along with a 10:30 reminder call.

"Thanks." Mike headed out of the east wing of the building where he and his staff resided, christened by the staff of Home Court Advantage as Duttonville, and made the track down the long corridor to the west wing of the building where Joshua's and his teams' offices were located, Key Town.

"Good morning, Mr. Dutton." Three women standing behind the large curved mahogany desk spoke almost in perfect harmony. Monica, the head receptionist, Amanda, a very pregnant brunette, and a new girl Mike didn't recognize. A beautiful, statuesque sister with nutmeg skin and high cheekbones. Either somebody in this girl's family was Asian, or she had an amazing hair weave. Looking into her almond-shaped eyes, he concluded that the former was true.

Mike flashed all three of the women a debonair smile. “Morning, ladies.” Mike held out his hand to the new statuesque sister. “I don’t believe we’ve met yet. I’m Michael Dutton.”

“Oh believe me, I know who you are. You’re The Man of Steel, arguably the best player ever in the history of the NBA. I’m Wendy Sars, and it is a pleasure, truly a pleasure, to finally meet you.” Wendy gushed, pumping Mike’s arm vigorously, while in the process revealing a large overbite.

Mike managed to ply his hand out of Wendy’s vice grip. “Well it’s nice to meet you, Ms. Cars.”

“No, not Cars, Sars, you know, like the virus. I’m half Chinese, but I’m totally clean.” Then the woman proceeded to laugh a laugh that would put Goofy to shame.

Mike shot questioning glances at Monica and Amanda. “Did either of you know that Ms. Sars here was a fan before you hired her?”

Amanda smiled nervously and glanced quickly over at the new girl. “It came up once or twice during the interview, however, Ms. Sars came highly recommended from the temp agency, and her last three employers gave her rave reviews. She’ll be with us through the fall, just until I return from my maternity leave.”

Mike's gaze landed on Monica, the one ultimately responsible for hiring new office personnel.

"She passed the psychological exam with flying colors," Monica said smoothly.

The psychological exam was something the company had to institute after a couple of run-ins with a few stalkers. Like the former in-house attorney, who out of the blue, after ten months of working for them, showed up to work one morning wearing a wedding dress with a mariachi band in tow, asking Mike to marry her. Or the poor sick woman, Joshua's former personal assistant, who had been caught on camera sneaking into the men's bathroom to collect Joshua's pee from one of the urinals. Mike pushed the image out of his head and smiled warmly at Home Court Advantage's newest employee. So far the psychological exam had been an excellent tool for weeding out the wackos.

"Nice meeting you, Wendy. I hope you enjoy your time here at Home Court Advantage." With that he bid the ladies a good day and proceeded down the hall. When Mike reached Key Town he knocked on the outer office door as he walked into the room. Selena, Joshua's very attractive, very single, and very sane, personal secretary regarded him warmly but professionally, when he entered the room.

"Hey, Selena."

"Hey, Mike."

"Where's my guy?"

She pointed to the closed office door. "He's been in there for the last two hours. I'm guessing he doesn't want to be disturbed because all his calls have been bouncing back out here to me."

He flashed Selena one of his most charming smiles. "Would you like me to check on him for you, milady?" Mike was a natural flirt who didn't mind flirting with women who weren't former fans of his ball playing days or madly in love with him. Selena responded with a slow sexy grin, just as brazen as the one he had given her. That's what he liked about her; she could give as good as she took.

"You're a prince among men, Michael. Would you do that for me?"

"I certainly would."

Mike rapped on Joshua's door before walking in. Joshua was standing in the large floor to ceiling picture window holding a sapphire necklace, staring out into the Texas skyline. The heaviness in his brother's heart seemed to weigh down the entire room. Joshua hadn't been the same since his wife and son left him five years ago. It was moments like these when Mike wished with all his heart that he could carry the heaviness for him.

Joshua turned and looked at Mike. "Hey bro, what's up?"

Mike took a seat on the couch in front of the fireplace. Their offices where almost exactly the same, except Mike's had been decorated with silver and blues, and Joshua's was decorated in gold and browns.

"I've been calling you all morning, and I keep getting Selena. She thought I should come in here and rescue you. You do know that your secretary's in love with you, right?" Mike shook his finger at his brother. "I told you not to hire Tyra Banks's cousin. You should have hired somebody matronly and saved like I did."

"Selena is saved."

"Yeah, but she's fine, Josh. Fine trumps saved any day of the week."

Joshua looked down at the necklace in his hand. "Naw, man. Not in my book it doesn't."

"Just trying to keep you honest, bro. Cause see with Mother Berry it's all about the job, no sexual tension in the workplace."

Joshua shook his head. "Seriously bro, it ain't like that."

"You sure?"

"Like it or not, I'm still married to Bella, right?"

"Who's the necklace for, Josh?"

"What? You think this is for, Selena?"

"Isn't it?"

"Naw, man. It's Bella's."

"You bought a necklace for a woman you haven't seen in five years. Did I miss something?"

Joshua sighed. "Yeah, a whole lot, you feel like grabbing a bite to eat?"

CHAPTER 8

Jabari bounced his basketball absentmindedly as he walked to the bus stop, crossing the ball with ease through his legs, thinking about home, his real home. This wasn't the first time they had run, but it had been the longest time they stayed. In the past, they'd never been gone more than a few days, a week tops before his dad found them and brought them back home again.

The last time they ran, Jabari had been six. He remembered his mother waking him up in the middle of the night, asking if he wanted to go on an adventure with her. They'd have to change their names she said, and wear disguises so no one would know who they were. How could any six-year-old boy resist?

"So who do you want to be, Jabari?" His mom asked, helping him into his rain boots and a makeshift terry cloth cape.

He was already wearing his Spiderman Underoos when she woke him, so he was already halfway dressed. Jabari looked down at the huge web on his Underoo pajamas he couldn't very well be Spiderman. Even six-year-olds knew that Spiderman didn't wear a cape. Jabari liked Spiderman cause he could spin really cool webs from his wrist, but as far as he was concerned, a guy really wasn't a superhero if he didn't have a cape.

"I'm Superfly," Jabari said confidently. His mom looked down at his costume like she wanted to laugh.

"Well, it's nice to meet you, Superfly. Can I ask why out of all the heroes in the world would you pick a garish stereotype from a 1970's blacksploitation film which thankfully you've never seen?"

"Huh?"

"Never mind, why, Superfly?"

"Oh, cause I can leap tall buildings with a single bound, and I don't get caught in spider webs when I do."

"I see," his mother said sounding impressed.

"See this big spider right here on my chest?"

"Yeah."

"This is like kryptonite to spider webs. When a spider web sees me flying by it just dissolves."

"What's your alias, Mr. Fly?"

"Mom, no. Not, Mr. Fly, Superfly."

"Sorry."

"What's an alias?"

"It's like a secret identity. You can't go around in your Superfly suit all the time. Can you?"

"No, just when I'm fighting crime."

"Exactly, so you'll need an everyday name then, like, Clark Kent." Jabari thought about this for a moment. Clark Kent was kind of dorky when he didn't have his Superman suit on. He kept bumping into things all the time. Jabari wanted to be cool whether he had his suit on or not. So he chose Matthew.

Matthew was the coolest kid in his class, and that was pretty hard to be when you were six. Matthew was white, with blonde hair and blue eyes, and all of the kids liked Matthew. His mom was never late picking him up, and she always looked happy. Matthew looked like everybody in his house always got along, and Jabari imagined that his mommy and daddy didn't fight late at night when they thought he was asleep, or that his mommy didn't cry into her pillow every night when his daddy was traveling for an away game.

Jabari thought about all of this and said, "I think I want to be called Matthew."

"Well it's very nice to meet you, Matthew. I think I'll call you Matt for short."

The game was fun for the first couple of days, but then he started to miss home. He missed his Grandma Mel, and Grandpa Jack, he missed his uncle Mike. He missed his bed and his room his daddy had decorated just like the Houston Rockets basketball court. Most importantly, Jabari missed his daddy.

Jabari lifted the ball up on his index finger and adroitly spun it the way he saw the Harlem Globe Trotters do on television. One day he was going to play in the NBA just like his daddy. Every day he honed his skills, playing pick-up games with Marcus and the older boys. He was getting better and better. Cause his dad would say, "You had to play the best if you wanted to be the best." One day, Jabari was going to play for the Houston Rockets, just like his pops. He'd enter the draft right after high school if he wasn't so sure his mother would have a complete conniption. Come to think of it, his pops probably wouldn't agree to that either. His mom was always telling him how important a good education was, how if he really wanted to be like his dad and his uncle, he needed to work hard in school. Cause they weren't dumb jocks. They both had college degrees. Uncle Mike even had his MBA. But Jabari hated everything about school, had ever since they got to New Orleans. In Texas, he had been at the top of his class. Granted he was six then, so how hard could it have been? Now, the only place he shined was on the basketball court. His math teacher, Mr. Keen, was constantly ragging on him, calling him an underachiever, saying how his test scores proved he was performing far below his ability. Mr. Keen would go into the same old song and dance about how a kid from the hood had a million and one chance of becoming a professional ball player. Jabari never listened. He figured he was a shoe-in, what with his skill, plus with both his dad and his uncle having played in the NBA. So what if Dad and Uncle Mike weren't related by blood? He might not have Uncle Mike's genes, but he certainly had his dad's.

When Mr. Keen started quoting all those bull statistics about black kids not being able to make it into the NBA, he wanted to say, "What about Joshua Keys and Michael Dutton?" Cause if the chances of a poor kid from the ghetto getting drafted was slim, the chance of two black kids raised on a ranch by white people, both going pro, and both being inducted into the hall of fame before the age of forty, had to be nearly impossible. But he couldn't say anything like that, because he'd promised his mom he wouldn't say anything to anybody that would cause people to start digging and figure out who they really were.

A promise was a promise, right? Outside of their house, he wasn't, Jabari Keys, Joshua Keys, former Houston Rockets Most Valuable Player's son. He was, Matthew LeBlanc, just another black boy growing up in the ghetto of New Orleans, without a father.

CHAPTER 9

Joshua had just finished his story and was waiting for his brother to respond. Mike was angry no doubt, but other than the uneaten breakfast plate in front of him, there would be no visual cues of his brother's irritation. Mike's handsome, chocolate features would remain smooth and relaxed, allowing any potential onlooker to see only what he wanted them to see, no more.

During his tenure as a professional ball player, Mike had earned the nickname, Man of Steel as well as the coveted position of team captain of the Houston Rockets, because of his uncanny ability to remain cool under pressure. The brothers would be described by almost anyone who knew them as kindred spirits, but in one regard they were complete opposites. Joshua wore his anger like a second skin. Mike wore his calm like military armor. Lately however, with the help of Christ, Joshua had begun the process of shedding that old skin. Some days were easier than others. Today wasn't one of those days. This was a day were he had to discuss Bella and anything related to his estranged wife at all was an emotional hot button. The whole world knew that by now, but nobody understood it better than his brother.

Mike stared at Joshua, his mask firmly in place, and Joshua thought about the one and only time in their adult lives were he had seen his brother, Michael Dutton, aka, the Man of Steel, lose his cool. Even then, Bella had been at the center of the controversy. Joshua shook his head as he recalled the incident. *Bella, it always came back to Bella.*

"What you gonna do, Josh?"

"I'm a get visitation with my son and reestablish a relationship with him."

"What about Bella?"

"What about her?"

Mike ignored the warning in Joshua's tone and pressed on anyway.

"What's the Big Man upstairs saying about that? He must be saying something. He prompted you to send the PI to New Orleans to look for her in the first place."

Joshua shook his head. "This time it's all about Jabari. Jabari's a child. Bella's a grown woman. She doesn't want to be married, and I'm done chasing after her. All I want now is a relationship with my son."

"You sure bout that?" Mike paused for a moment allowing his question room to sink in before he spoke again. "Most importantly, are you sure that's what God wants?"

The look of agonizing defeat showed clearly on Joshua's face. Unlike his brother, he was no master of hiding his emotions.

"Look bro, I'm on your side. Always believe that. And as much as I want to hate Bella for everything, I don't. I can't. I know you can't either. She's family."

Family was important to Joshua, for sure, but it was downright holy to Michael. Mike's birth mother was an addict. When Mike was three, she'd sold him to an undercover police officer for a fix. After being shuffled from one irresponsible family member to the next, Mike came to live in the foster care of the Kennedys. It was there that he took one look at Joshua, who was just beginning to toddle and declared him to be 'my baby brother.' A blood brother could never have been more loyal.

Years later, when Mike's addicted birth mother came looking for her multi-millionaire son, Mike didn't kick her to the curb like most people would have, like Joshua certainly would have. Mike put her in a rehab program and got her some help, or at least tried to get her some help, until it became crystal clear she didn't want any. Mike didn't talk about his birth mother at all. Still, Joshua was almost certain his brother kept in contact with the woman. For no other reason than because she was family.

"Don't get me wrong, I'm mad as hell at her for taking Jabari and jetting the way she did, but I love her, and I know you still love her too. That's got to count for something, right? All these good looking women after you, not just the skanks— the sanctified ones too, but God puts love in your heart for Bella. If God didn't want you to love this woman, Josh, couldn't he have taken those feelings away?"

Joshua didn't tell Mike just how often he had prayed for God to do just that. Remove the longing he felt in his heart for this woman. Bella was constantly in his prayers. He had learned early in his walk with the Lord that you couldn't harbor hatred in your heart for someone you were constantly praying for. You had no other choice but to love them.

"All I'm saying, Josh, is keep your heart open to whatever the Big Man is telling you about all this."

Joshua's face softened. "You sure you not the preacher in this family?"

"You've definitely cornered the market on that one. So stop tryin' to change the subject."

Joshua smirked. "Yeah, whatever man, you sure sound like a preacher to me."

"Alright, I'm a leave it alone, cause I know you hear me."

"Yeah, I hear you," Joshua said, rising to pay the bill. "Anything else, Bishop Jakes?"

"Yeah, call your mother. She says she's been dreaming about you a lot. She's threatening to come out here if she don't hear from you soon."

Joshua laughed. "Mel's trippin'. I just spoke to her a week ago."

"I'm not playin', Josh. If she comes out here, she not stayin' with me. She is gonna be at your house, washing and ironing your drawers."

"Okay, okay, I'll call her. You coming to Bible Study tonight?"

"That depends, you teaching?"

Joshua grinned. "Yeah."

"Then, I'll be there."

CHAPTER 10

"Mrs. Keys?"

"Yes." It was the second time in twenty four hours that Bella had answered to that name.

"I'm Jordan Copperhead, I'm going to be representing Mr. Keys in the custody matter today, as well as the subsequent divorce proceedings." Bella looked around the hallway expectantly.

"Where's Joshua?"

"Just so you know Mr. Keys' main concern today is getting this visitation situation worked out. Are you opposed to my client having weekends, summers, and rotating holidays?"

"Well, I don't know. Can you tell me where Joshua is?"

"Mr. Keys won't be here today. Now, I've handled tons of these cases and I can tell you this: Everything goes smoothly if we can work through all the details out here. Then I'll go before the judge, present the agreed upon motion, and presto, we're done. We can be in and out of here in twenty minutes. You can go back to your life, and I can make my morning flight back to Houston. Do we have a deal? I spotted some television cameras outside, no doubt some beat reporter got wind of all this. So there's no need for us to be combative or argumentative with each other. I say we do our best to agree. So, how do weekends, summers, and rotating holidays sound to you?"

Somewhere along the line Bella had stopped listening. She was too stung by the realization that Joshua had not come for her. *He's not coming this time. He's not coming.* Suddenly Bella's hands were shaking, and she felt herself blinking back tears. Jordan Copperhead waved his hand in front of Bella's face like it was a magic wand.

"Hello, earth to Mrs. Keys. Shall we go inside and do this for the cameras." Bella nodded her head slowly, but she didn't move.

"Mrs. Keys?" A matronly black woman came up to Bella and put her hand on her shoulder.

"Yes?"

"I'm, Miriam Blackwell. Mr. Keys has retained me to look after your best interest in these court proceedings."

Bella and Jordan Copperhead both gasped at the same time.

"He hired you?" the attorney asked incredulously. "I can't believe this."

"Wait a minute, so what are you saying? That Josh is paying you, too?" Bella asked.

"That is correct, ma'am," Miriam said.

Bella began to feel herself become unglued. "So you work for him, right? I mean, basically he has two attorneys, and I ain't got nobody. He didn't have to do this. I would have let him see, Jabari."

"Let me be very clear about this, Mrs. Keys. I work for you. Mr. Keys has retained me to look out for your best interest in this matter. Our meetings are totally confidential. What we discuss is between you and I. I am bound by oath to fight completely on your behalf, just as Mr. Keys', attorney here, is bound by law to represent him. Doesn't matter who's paying my bill. As unorthodox as that sounds—I'll admit, even to me. But if you feel this compromises my position, I'll be happy to recommend another attorney for you."

Bella studied the older woman in front of her, she had a calming demeanor, and an honest face and since this was entirely within the realm of something Joshua would do, Bella decided to trust the woman. *This is a fight*, he was telling her, *but I'm gon fight fair.* "That won't be necessary." Bella said. "I believe you."

Miriam Blackwell locked eyes with Joshua's attorney. "Good. Then from this moment on, Mr. Copperhead will be communicating directly with me."

"Fine, my client wants every weekend," Jordan said.

"My client is a single mother, who works during the week. Weekends should be split." Miriam looked at Bella. "Every other weekend, does that sound reasonable?" Bella nodded her head.

"Granted," Jordan said.

"And child support." Miriam said.

"My client is offering child support and a generous maintenance allowance both to begin immediately. However, in return he wants unrestricted phone privileges with his son, beginning tonight." Jordan Copperhead handed Miriam a business card with Joshua's contact information on it.

"Mrs. Keys, can you see to that?" Miriam asked. Again Bella nodded her head yes.

"What time will Jabari be calling?" Jordan Copperhead asked. He was speaking to Bella, but he made a point, Bella noticed, to look at Miriam. So she followed his example and spoke to Miriam as well. "We don't have long distance, but he can call from my neighbor's phone at around seven o'clock tonight."

"Fine, Mr. Keys will be awaiting Jabari's call at 7:00 PM sharp. Anything else, Ms. Blackwell?" Jordan said.

"When we go before the judge this morning, I'm going to suggest that we meet here again in three months, for a status check. But in the meantime, Mrs. Keys, is there anything else you need?"

"I can't pay my rent, I told my landlord I'd have the money for him today."

Jordan Copperhead sighed. He pulled out his cellular phone and walked away to make a call, presumably to Joshua. A few minutes later he returned to say that the money would be wired to her account before the end of the day. Forty minutes later they were done. She should have been happy, right? He was finally giving her what she wanted, her freedom. So why wasn't she happy? Why did she feel like she was dying? Bella thanked Miriam Blackwell as they walked out of the courthouse. She tried to lift her head but it felt like a twenty pound weight.

CHAPTER 11

Jabari was peering out the window, daydreaming when he almost missed his stop. If it hadn't been for seeing Marcus's long legs cut across the old courtyard down the street from their building, he would have missed it completely. Instead, at the last minute, Jabari signaled the driver who made an uncharacteristic stop in the middle of the street, but not without reprimanding Jabari and telling him to pay closer attention next time.

"Yo, Marcus, wait up!" Jabari called.

But the older boy was already out of ear range. Although they rode the same bus every day, Jabari never sat next to Marcus or any of Marcus's friends, because Jabari was only a sixth grader, and Marcus was in high school. In fact, other than a slight non-committal chin lift in his direction every now and again, Marcus never acknowledged Jabari in public, unless, they were on the basketball court. Basketball was the great equalizer. Jabari's shorter legs tried to catch up with Marcus. He had to run just to keep the older boy in sight. Jabari turned the corner just in time to see Marcus disappear through a door into one of the old boarded-up abandoned buildings.

"Marcus? You in here?" Jabari knew it wasn't safe to be here. Drug dealers and addicts did their business here. His mom would have a heart attack if she found out he was anywhere near this place. He'd seen enough crime in his neighborhood to know that if people were desperate enough, they'd steal anything, from anybody. Jabari felt his throat go dry.

"Yo, Marcus. You in here?" he whispered. Jabari stopped. He heard voices. Peering through a hole in the wall, he saw Marcus and his mother Belinda. Belinda was sitting on the floor leaning up against the wall. Her hair was matted and a long string of spittle dripped from the side of her mouth.

"We ain't seen you in over a week. Where you get the money this time? You already sold my shoes. The TV."

"I ain't stole nothing," Belinda slurred. "Terry helped me. He real good to me."

"Look at you." Marcus spat. "He ain't good to you." Belinda's head slumped forward.

Marcus knelt beside her. He lifted her eyelid and gently tapped her face, "Ma, Ma, wake up."

He reached into his book bag and pulled out a sandwich. "You gotta eat."

Belinda batted him away like a bothersome housefly. "My stomach can't take it. Just leave, Marcus. Leave me alone. You blowing my high."

Marcus stood and stared down at her. "When you coming home? Grandma's worried bout you." But Belinda was already asleep. Deciding that this probably wasn't the best time to have a conversation with Marcus, Jabari tried to back slowly out the building as quietly as possible, but his pants leg snagged a raised floorboard in the doorway. Jabari tumbled backwards out into the courtyard. Marcus was on him in a flash. He grabbed Jabari up by the collar and pulled him off the ground.

"What you doing here, shorty?"

"I saw you go in and I just wanted to—" Jabari stuttered. "I wanted to show you something."

"Don't ever let me catch you round here! You heard? Ever! Don't even walk this way! From now on you cut through the yard."

"But Mr. Terry don't like for me to cut through his yard."

"Man, screw him." Marcus growled.

Marcus hated the landlord with a passion, now Jabari knew why.

"You think he cares if one of these hypes knock you upside your head and kill you?"

"No," Jabari said quietly.

"That's right. He don't! Cause he don't care bout nobody but himself."

"I saw you walk this way when I got off the bus, I just wanted to show you something," Jabari explained.

Marcus stared at Jabari, like he was trying to gauge how much he had seen and overheard. Jabari kept his face as innocent looking as possible.

"Come on," Marcus said after a few moments, "let's get out of here. What you want to show me?"

"My dad's here, my mom had to go to court today." Jabari pulled a crumbled magazine picture out his back pack and handed it to Marcus. "I got this out the school library today. See, that's my dad, and that's my mom."

"This says her name is Bella Rose."

"Yeah, but I told you my mom made us change our names so nobody would find us."

"Okay, shorty, that kinda look like your moms, but where you at?"

Jabari hadn't thought about that. He shrugged. "I don't know if I was born yet. But if I was, I don't think my dad would've wanted me in the limelight.

Man, everybody knows, Bad Boy Joshua Keys hates the media."

Marcus chuckled and nodded his head. "True that. Okay, shorty, I believe you. But why you care so much about what people think? Long as you know the truth, that's all that matters."

"I only told you," Jabari mumbled, feeling not vindicated, as he had hoped, but kind of silly.

"You a cool little dude, and your moms is a pretty nice lady. I hope your dad does find you and takes you outta this hellhole."

In the five years they had been living in New Orleans Jabari hadn't made any friends. He hadn't bothered to, hoping every day that his father would find him and take him back to his real life. He realized Marcus was the best friend—well maybe not friend, that was obviously too strong a word, but whatever it was, Marcus was the best he had. They had a lot in common. Marcus had lost his mama. Jabari had lost his daddy and they both loved basketball. When they reached the front porch of their apartment, Jabari scanned the street looking for an expensive vehicle. "My mom and dad are probably on their way back from court, would you like to come in and meet him?"

"Not this time, shorty. Tell him hi for me though." Marcus palmed Jabari's head and walked inside the building.

CHAPTER 12

When Bella walked out of the courthouse that afternoon she saw the repo man driving away with her car. That snake, Terry must have tipped him off. The irony was that now, of course, with the money Joshua would be giving her in child support, she could actually pay the note.

Bella took the bus to the bank where she discovered that Joshua had wired $3500 into her account. She had no idea how she would get to the market now, but she decided she had until Monday to figure it all out. She would take tomorrow off because now that she had to split weekends with Joshua, she wanted to spend as much time with Jabari as possible. Bella took a cab to the grocery store and paid the driver extra to wait for her. She knew Jabari would be disappointed when he found out Joshua wasn't in the city, and she wanted to soften the blow by having all his favorite foods waiting for him. With any luck, he was still at the playground playing basketball with Marcus and the other boys. That would give her time to prepare the food.

You've waited this long. She practiced to herself in the cab on the way home. *You can wait one more week to see your dad.*

❧

Jabari ran out of the building at full speed when he saw Bella getting out of the cab with the bags. "Where's dad? Is he on his way?"

"Honey, come help me with the bags."

Jabari ran up beside her and kissed her cheek. "Sorry, Mom." He scooped up five plastic bags in each hand and ran back up the stairs. Bella paid the driver and walked up the stairs to the apartment, dreading the conversation with her son.

CHAPTER 13

Houston, Texas, Friday night, Aug. 25, 2005

If anyone ever doubted Joshua Keys' conversion, and the media certainly gave it pause, they had only to look at the before and after snapshots of Joshua's life. Joshua's world used to consist of frequent bar fights and various other scrimmages on and off court. In fact, Joshua Keys had more fines and lawsuits than anyone else in the history of the NBA. He had slowed down a bit when he married Bella Rose, the beautiful young daughter of a pastor he had met at a revival, but when she revealed to him that she was pregnant by another man, the fighting and drinking started up again.

Today, Joshua was the newest pastoral staff member at New Horizons Christian Training Center. He had come so far in such a short amount of time, some days he could hardly believe the transformation himself. As one of five assistant pastors, it was Joshua's duty to teach the Foundational Truth classes for new members, as well as occasionally step in for his head pastor and mentor, Bishop Micah Ford, and preach Sunday morning services.

Joshua closed his Bible and stuffed his notes into his briefcase. He had just concluded his thirty minute lecture from the book of Romans. He had broken the participants of his Foundational Truths Class into small groups, given them their assignment, and instructed them to close in prayer at the conclusion of class. He looked up to see Selena patiently waiting for him.

"Hey Pastor, that was a wonderful lecture, too bad I only got to hear the tail end of it."

Selena had recently joined New Horizons and given her life to Christ. She hadn't really connected with many people in the church yet, so Joshua had suggested she join the Foundational Truths class. Joshua knew that in a church this size, it was easy to get lost. That was one of the reasons he loved teaching Foundational Truths, he watched many people form lasting relationships throughout the class. Joshua knew it was these kinds of connections that kept members from falling through the cracks.

So far, Selena appeared to be shy and slow in forming friendships with other women. The men however, seemed to gravitate towards her. She paid little attention to them though, and kept her eyes glued on Joshua and every word that came out his mouth. Joshua looked around the room for a group for Selena to join.

"It's okay, I'm not staying tonight for the discussion."

Joshua frowned. "Why not?"

Selena hunched her shoulders. "If you're not staying, I don't really see the point."

Joshua thought about this for a moment then reasoned she probably felt this way because she didn't really know too many people in the class yet.

"Besides," Selena added quickly, "I said I'd have that Moyer report on your desk first thing Monday morning, and I didn't get to it today. I plan to work on it all weekend."

"I appreciate your dedication to the company, Selena, but the Moyer report can wait."

"Really?"

"Yes, relax this weekend. In fact, take Monday off too."

"Wow, for real?"

"My brother and I do not pay you enough to take work home on the weekends."

Selena laughed. "Now that you mention it, I have been wanting to visit my aunt in South Carolina."

"Do that. Take Tuesday and Wednesday off too. Nobody wants to come back to work jetlagged."

"Wow, thank you, Joshua. That's very generous of you."

"You're welcome."

"I guess since I'm officially on vacation, I could stay tonight—that is, if you really want me too."

"I really want you to. You'll get more out of the Bible study if you participate in the discussion. I'd be staying myself if I didn't have another engagement."

"You mean a date?"

Joshua lifted his eyebrow and Selena blushed.

"I'm sorry, that was way out of line. I shouldn't have asked about your personal affairs."

Joshua chuckled. "No, it's alright. It's a date with my son. I'll be speaking with him by telephone tonight."

"But I thought, you hadn't spoken to them in years."

"The man, who came to the office the other day was a private detective. I've found them."

Michael sauntered over to the two of them. "Good to see you in the house of the Lord, Sister Selena."

Selena laughed. "Good to see you too, Brother Michael."

"I hope you're planning on staying, we need a fourth person for our group."

"As a matter of fact I am."

Mike locked eyes with Joshua, over Selena's head. "Don't you have somewhere to be?"

Joshua gave Mike a fist pound and headed out the door.

CHAPTER 14

New Orleans, Sunday, Aug. 28, 2005

Bella sat in the small kitchen drinking a cup of mint tea, trying to settle her stomach. From her position at the table she could see Jabari sitting in the living room watching television. Jabari hadn't said one word about his conversation with his dad all weekend. He'd actual broken down and cried Friday when he found out that Josh wasn't coming. It was the first time Bella realized the awful extent of what she had put her son through. And for what, her pride?

"Ma, they've been doing this all day," Jabari called.

Bella walked into the tiny living room and took a seat on the edge of the couch. A weather alert had interrupted his television program again.

"Don't worry, honey, that's pretty standard with these kinds of storms."

Bella had been born and raised in New Orleans. She knew all about the anxiety and panic that swept over the city moments before a storm.

"So, how was your conversation with your dad, Friday?" Bella said, trying to take his mind off the storm.

Jabari kept his eyes glued to the television. "Fine."

Bella waited for him to elaborate, but Jabari said nothing more. "Just fine?"

"No, actually it was more like, good, real good." Jabari tore his eyes away from the TV screen and looked at her then. His eyes held the tiniest glint of amusement. "Why? You wanna know what we talked about?"

"No, that's your private business between you and your father."

"You don't even want to know what Dad said about you?"

Bella stiffened. "I would never have agreed to let him talk to you, if I'd known he'd be bad-mouthing me."

Jabari looked at her with disgust. "He didn't even say nothing. I was just playing."

Ding! Just like that, the match was over. Each one of them retreated to their separate corners. Bella went back to her seat at the kitchen table. Jabari went back to watching television.

Bella knew her son. Every since they'd left Houston, Jabari had considered himself to be the man of the house. He was still upset that he had broken down in front of her. He had been inconsolable until she told him that his dad would be eagerly awaiting his call at seven o'clock sharp that night. She'd spoken to Maggie Trendale and asked if Jabari could use their phone.

Actually, she'd asked if Matt could call his dad, because since they'd moved here Matt and Rosemary where the names they went by. Jabari came into the kitchen and sat down in the chair opposite her.

"Ma, Mayor Nagin's on the television, he telling everyone they have to leave the city. I think we ought to go."

"Matt—"

"You said you wouldn't call me that at home."

"Sorry, my bad. I was just . . ." She had only made the mistake because she was thinking about the lie she had told Maggie, the closest friend she had since returning to New Orleans. How every time Maggie called her Rosemary instead of Bella she felt like she was lying.

"Jabari, evacuations cost money."

"You said Dad wired you some money."

"That was to pay Terry his rent and to buy groceries. We just went to court on Friday. I haven't started getting any child support money yet."

"Well did you pay him already?"

"Who?"

"Mr. Terry," Jabari said, clearly exasperated.

"Yes and the rest of that money is for booth fees."

"If New Orleans gets sucked away in a hurricane, you won't need no money for booth fees. We need to use that money for gas. Get in the car and drive to Houston. Daddy still lives in Houston, right?"

"Yes. Your dad still lives in Houston."

Jabari pointed to the TV. "Ma, look at all these people leaving."

Bella watched the television footage of long lines of people leaving the city, filling up at the gas pumps, and stocking up on water. She didn't dare tell him the real reason they couldn't leave, that her car had been repossessed; it would only underscore the life that he was missing with Joshua. A life she had robbed him of.

"You know what my daddy use to say? He said people left because they didn't have any faith. He was wrong about a lot of things. But never about storms."

"You think they're staying?"

"Are you kidding me? The Right Reverend and First Lady LeBlanc? My daddy's probably speaking to the storm right now, commanding the winds and the waves to be still. We'll ride out the storm tonight. If things get too bad, we'll go to the Superdome tomorrow. Okay?"

Jabari reached over and kissed her forehead.

"What's that for?"

"That was from Dad. He said to give his beautiful Bella a kiss."

CHAPTER 15

Houston, Monday, Aug. 29, 2005

NO!" Joshua, sat up in bed with a start. Sweat glistened from his body. His heart slammed violently against his ribcage. The bedside alarm clock read 3:00 AM. Joshua jumped out of bed and fell to his knees. "Keep them safe, Jesus!" he begged. "Keep them safe!"

This had become somewhat of a ritual. At least two to three times a week for the past three months Joshua had been awakened with nightmares of Bella and Jabari's demise. Dreams of Bella being murdered violently in a brothel in the French Quarter, dreams of Jabari left to fend for himself on the streets of New Orleans, forced to join a gang for survival. Tonight, Joshua dreamed of Bella and Jabari being washed away by a great flood, their swollen bodies half eaten by crocodiles as they floated aimlessly over Lake

Pontchartrain. Each time he was awakened with one of these horrible visions, Joshua did the same thing he was doing right now: fell to his knees and prayed. Premonitions of his family's destruction are what prompted him to send a private eye to New Orleans to look for Bella and Jabari in the first place. Because of the strained relationship Bella had with her folks, the last place he'd assume she'd ever return to was there. Still, night after night, the vivid dreams he had seemed to suggest otherwise. So Joshua hired Mattingham and sent him to search for them there.

Joshua grabbed the Bible off the nightstand and flipped the pages quickly to the 91st Psalm, even though he knew the passage by heart. Joshua clasped the Bible and prayed fervently.

"He who dwells in the shelter of the Most High, will rest in the shadow of the Almighty. I will say of the Lord, He is my refuge and my fortress, my God in whom I trust. Surely he will save you from the fowler's snare and from the deadly pestilence. He will cover you with his feathers, and under his wings you will find refuge. Cover them under your feathers, Lord Jesus. Please cover them," Joshua pleaded.

Joshua had expected the dreams to stop once Mattingham had actually found his family. He thought that the peace that had come over him when he'd spoken to his accountant on Friday and learned that money had indeed been wired into Bella's account—so she wouldn't be doing God knows what, just to make ends meet—he thought that peace would remain. He'd thought there would be a permanent settling of his spirit once he heard the sound of Jabari's voice later on that same night. The first time he had heard the sound in five years. The phone rang just as his attorney said it would at seven o'clock sharp. Joshua, not wanting to miss out on another minute with his son, answered on the first ring.

"Hello."

"Hey, Dad, it's me, Jabari."

"Oh, man, it's so good to hear your voice. How are you, son?"

"Better now, I guess."

"Better? Why? You weren't sick were you? Is your mama hurt?"

"Naw, we good, Dad. It's just— I mean, it's kind of silly now. I don't want you gettin' the wrong impression about me. I don't want you thinkin' you raised no little punk."

Pain gripped Joshua's heart, at the thought of his son, forced into manhood long before season. "I'm your dad and you know I love you, right?"

"Yeah."

"Then know this, there is nothing you could ever say or do that would ever make me think that about you."

"Ma told me not to get my hopes up, but I kinda had it in my head that you were gon be here when I got home from school. But when I got back, and you wasn't here. I was really upset. I broke down in front of Ma. I cried like a little chump."

"Crying because you're disappointed doesn't make you a chump, Jabari. Real men can cry."

"I ain't never seen you cry."

Joshua thought about the example he had set for his son and millions of other American youth during his tenure as a professional basketball player. He had gained the nickname Bad Boy Joshua Keys because he had only known how to show two emotions on and off the court, joy and anger. He knew he was largely responsible for Jabari's lopsided outlook on manhood. "Believe it or not, I'm crying now."

"For real?"

"Yep," Joshua chuckled. "I can't help it, man. I love you so much. I'm happy to hear your voice, but I'm also disappointed because all this time I haven't been able to hold you and tell you how much you mean to me. I haven't been able to hang out with you, or play ball with you. Or, you know, just do dad stuff, like talk to you about girls." Joshua ran his hand over his face and cleared his throat. "So, what's up, little man, you got a girlfriend yet or what?"

"There's this one girl, she's in high school. Her name is Keisha. I kind of like her, but as far she's concerned, I don't even exist. But Dad, you should see my three pointer! Even Marcus says it's sweet. You think it's genetic?"

Joshua swallowed a familiar knot. "Could be."

Joshua heard a female voice in the background.

"Okay, ma'am, I will," Jabari said. "Uh, Dad, I have to go now. We don't have long distance, and I'm on our neighbors' phone."

"Jabari, you have my number now. I want you to memorize it."

"Okay, Dad, I will."

"Call me anytime, day or night. You don't have to wait to call me from the neighbors' phone. You can call me collect right from your house phone. Just dial zero, and have the operator put you through. I'll see you in seven days, alright? A car will pick you up and take you to the airport right after school."

"I know. Ma told me. Uh, Dad, before you go, Mr. Trendale's sitting right here. He's a really big fan. He wants to talk to you."

"Sure thing, sport. Give, Bella-the-beautiful a kiss for me, alright?" Joshua didn't know why he had added that last part but he had. The words were out, and he couldn't take them back.

"Okay, Dad, I will. I love you."

"His faithfulness will be your shield and rampart. You will not fear the terror of night, nor the arrow that flies by day, nor the pestilence that stalks in the darkness, nor the plague that destroys at midday. A thousand may fall at your side, ten thousand at your right hand, but it will not come near you. You will only observe with your eyes and see the punishment of the wicked." Joshua grabbed a fistful of bed sheet and fought back the unbidden tears.

"If you make the Most High your dwelling even the Lord, who is my refuge, then no harm will befall you, no disaster will come near your tent. He will command his angels concerning you." Joshua felt power surge through his entire being when he spoke those last seven little words, so he repeated them over and over again.

"He will command his angels concerning you. He will command his angels concerning you, Bella! He will command his angels concerning you, Jabari, to guard you in all your ways! They will lift you up in their hands, so that you will not strike your foot against a stone. You will tread upon the lion and the cobra; you will trample the great lion and the serpent. Because he loves me, says the, Lord, I will rescue him; I will protect him, for he acknowledges my name. He will call upon me and I will answer him; I will be with him in trouble, I will deliver him and honor him. With long life will I satisfy him and show him my salvation."

Joshua gripped the sides of the bed and held on, like an ancient Hebrew priest of old, holding onto the horns of the altar, he held on. "Your salvation. Lord, please, your salvation. My son and my wife aren't saved. They don't know you. They can't die and not know you. They just can't."

NEW ORLEANS
1996

CHAPTER 16

Officer Timothy O'Brien scanned the faces of the women who had been swept up in the prostitution bust. Silently he grieved for each of them. His eyes fell on a fair skinned African American, more child-like than woman. He estimated her age, eighteen, nineteen tops. She was dressed for the part, but her presence was somehow incongruous here. She didn't fit. As he moved closer to get a better look, Tim felt his heart turn a somersault inside his chest. Could this be her, his angel? He had dreamed of meeting her again. He thought it would be at a crusade where she'd be preaching the Gospel to millions, but never, never, in a in his wildest dreams, did he'd ever imagine her in a place like this.

"Bella? Bella LeBlanc?" Tim called. The girl's head snapped up at the sound of the name. Just for a millisecond, a small spark of life flickered beneath the surface of her brown eyes. But the moment passed just as quickly as it had come, and all that was left was a hopeless stare.

Tim spoke to the senior officer in charge, "Hobbs, I know that girl."

"You know her, or you'd like to know her?" the pug faced officer said with a smirk.

"It's not what you think. Please, release her to me."

"I don't know, Officer Goody. She's pretty feisty. Four of my men had to chase that one three blocks. She might be a little too much for you to handle, first time out the starting gate, but then again, what do I know, maybe you church boys like it ruff." Officer Hobbs grinned roguishly at O'Brien, the four other police officers present laughed on cue.

O'Brien walked around back and opened the trunk of his squad car, looking for something, anything to cover her near nakedness. He breathed a sigh of relief when he found an old red wool blanket he'd long forgotten about. *Red's good,* he thought, *for the blood.* His head was swimming with a thousand questions and a thousand more revelations. *She's the reason, isn't she? Why you told me to turn my back on the pastorate, join the force instead.* By the time O'Brien walked back around to the front of his squad car, his easy-going carefree demeanor was gone. All the muscles in his body tensed for the unexpected, and when he spoke this time, it was with the courage and conviction of a man who understood his purpose. "What's it going to be, Hobbs? Are you going to release her to me or not?"

❧

Officer Hobbs studied the younger man standing in front of him. O'Brien had come from a prominent clergy family in New Orleans. Unlike most guys on the force, O'Brien didn't even need this job. Why he had become a police officer in the first place nobody had figured out. But what they did know, was that Timothy O'Brien was single handedly responsible for introducing one third of the New Orleans PD to Jesus the Christ. Thanks to O'Brien, Hobbs had lost some of his best drinking buddies. Hobbs was teasing the man, but he knew that O'Brien had some noble cause for wanting to set the young girl free.

"Tell me one thing. Why do you care?" Hobbs asked.

"She doesn't belong here."

"What's in it for me?"

"Come on, Jack, you know I'm not out here soliciting sexual favors."

Hobbs shrugged, "Doesn't matter if you're boning them or saving their souls. Every man gotta pay, O'Brien. So I'm asking you, if I do this for you, what's in it for me?"

Suddenly, the words were like a fire in the pit of O'Brien's belly. Before he could censor them, take control of them, the words rolled off his tongue and exploded into the air. "Trust me when I tell you that her Father is somebody you don't want to mess with. If you release her to me, it would mean that your wife won't wake a widow tomorrow, and that your kids won't grow up without you. How's that for a favor, Hobbs?"

O'Brien's words hit the lead officer with so much force they stole his breath. And the feeling that came over him, well, there was no other way to say it, except to say that Hobbs felt the hand of death. In a city like New Orleans where black magic was real—not made-for-television-real, but kill-you-and-everybody-in-your-family-including-the-dog-real. Hobbs decided that he better not take any chances. For all he knew, she could be the daughter of a witch doctor, a shaman, or a voodoo high priest. Officer Hobbs unlinked the girl from the others and handed her to O'Brien.

"I'd keep her cuffed if I were you. Like I said, she's a runner."

O'Brien threw the blanket around the girl and put her in the back of his squad car.

"Hey, O'Brien," a young rookie called. "Don't forget to wear a hat!"

O'Brien dismissed the guy with a wave. It didn't matter what any of them thought. All that mattered to him now was getting his angel out of there.

CHAPTER 17

When he had driven about a mile or so, O'Brien spotted a small neighborhood park and pulled his squad car over to the side of the road. "I can't believe I actually said that. Heck, I can't believe he actually bought it."

"Bought what?" she mumbled from the back of his cab.

O'Brien turned his body around so that he faced the girl. "The lead officer back there, he wanted me to pay him for your release. I told him what the Spirit told me to say, 'Your Father is extremely powerful, that He wouldn't hesitate to kill him if he didn't let you go.'"

"He powerful, alright, too chicken-hearted to kill." She yawned. "Might pay somebody to do it though."

"I wasn't talking about your earthly father, Bella. I was speaking of your heavenly one. Don't you get it? It doesn't matter what turns you took in life, how you got to this point, the Father has decided to redeem you. I wasn't even supposed to be on duty today. Heck, I'm not even supposed to be on the force. I'm supposed to be in seminary school. He orchestrated all of this for you. Your heavenly Father loves you so much that He would have killed that man back there if he would have tried to interfere with the redemption plan He has for you."

A mixture of bitterness and anger contorted her face. "You don't know me, and you definitely don't know my daddy. So we can dispense with all the pleasantries, 'Mr. Serve and Protect'. Just so you know, I don't do nothing for free. Not even for a Get Out of Jail Card. You want me, you pay, like everybody else. And if you thinking about taking it, think again. Nobody takes anything from me anymore."

Her words, laced with so much anger and so much pain pierced Tim's heart, but he tucked them away for safekeeping. Later he would cry out in supplication before the Almighty God for her. He would petition Him for her recompense, for every horrible thing that had ever been done.

"I don't want anything from you, Bella, I'm just returning the favor, one life for another."

"I don't know what you talkin' about."

"You really don't remember me, do you? Twelve years ago, you saved my life."

She stared at him blankly.

"Timmy O'Brien. Bible Camp for PK's." He reached into his back pocket and removed a worn, creased photo from his wallet. A picture of a green-eyed boy in a wheelchair and a little buttercup girl with pig tails. The little girl's arm hung protectively around the boy's shoulder.

"I have hair now," O'Brien said, pointing to his now healthy head full of reddish-brown hair. "Back then I had leukemia. That summer was supposed to be my last. My organs had started to shut down, and the doctors had pretty much sent me home to die. But you laid hands on me and told me Jesus wanted to heal me. I've been cancer free ever since. "

"Get that out of my face!" she growled.

"Bella—"

"My name is Rosemary! So don't go mixing up who I am now with who I used to be."

"I just told you that you laid hands on me and through the power of God, you healed me of cancer. Cancer. Doesn't that mean anything to you?"

"I still lay hands, Timmy, just not in the way you think," she spoke in a low sultry voice. Tim's face turned bright red and the girl cackled with laughter. Tim turned his body so that he was facing forward in his seat. He turned the key in the ignition, pulled the car out into traffic and from memory, headed in the direction of the LeBlanc home.

"It's obvious to me that you've forgotten who you are. So let me tell you what I remember. I remember an eight-year-old girl, on fire for God and totally in love with her Christ. You used to tell me, well . . . you used to tell all of us kids at camp, that just because our fathers were preachers that didn't mean we were gonna make it into heaven. You said that we had to know God for ourselves. You said our daddy's God couldn't be our God. Your dad was such a hero to you. You had us convinced that Reverend LeBlanc was like . . . Superman or something. We thought he could fly. You used to say that your daddy was the best preacher in the south and you were going to grow up to be an even better preacher then he was, because God had called you to a chosen generation. You were my Joshua, Bella. You led me into the promised land of my healing. I waited for you to return that next summer and every summer after that. But you never came back."

As Tim locked eyes with her through the rearview mirror, heavy tears fell from his green eyes as he unapologetically wept. "What happened to you?"

"Kryptonite," she said. She pulled the red blanket around her shoulder and fell asleep.

CHAPTER 18

Tim led Bella up the walkway of the professionally manicured lawn, and rang the doorbell of the pristine Greek Revival Georgian-style manor. There was the sound of heavy footsteps, then Reverend LeBlanc's large, imposing frame stood in the doorway. The minister's glance landed briefly on Tim, then he took in his daughter in her entirety. The sheer revulsion and disgust radiating from the minister caused Tim instinctually to shift his body weight shielding Bella from her father's eyes.

"Sylvia!" Reverend LeBlanc bellowed.

Mrs. LeBlanc materialized beside her husband in an instant.

"Oh, Bella, we've been worried sick about you!" she shuffled her daughter quickly into the house and up the long spiral staircase. This reaction also struck Tim as wrong, but at least there was a hint of kindness to the woman's voice. Even if it did ring false. Not your typical prodigal's welcome home.

Lord. I have no right to judge them. Help me to see with your eyes, and to listen with your ears.

As Tim balanced his club soda on his knee, and watched Reverend LeBlanc pace back and forth across the floor of his mahogany wood paneled office, he found himself wondering if his prayer had been heard at all. The more the Reverend LeBlanc spoke, the more anxious Tim found himself becoming. Right now, the famous televangelist's words were setting off a five-star alarm in his spirit.

"We've prayed over her. I've tried to drive it out. She'll do well for a while and then all of a sudden she'll just disappear. We haven't seen her in two weeks. After much prayer and fasting on the matter, I've come to understand that there is no cure for conditions like these, only prayer for the grace to endure."

Prayer for the grace to endure? What about King Nebuchadnezzar, he ate grass for seven years. God restored him? What about the demon possessed man who lived among the tombs, Jesus healed him. That kid, the one that had the demon that kept throwing him into the fire. What about him? These would all be classified as mental illnesses today, right?

"I liken myself to the apostle Paul," Reverend LeBlanc said, interrupting Tim's thoughts. "Though he had healed many, he was given a thorn in his side. A messenger of Satan, to keep him humble, because of the awesome power of God at work in his life. Bella is my thorn."

Tim cocked his head and stared up at the man of God standing before him. *Huh, Jesus, did he really just compare his daughter to a messenger of Satan?*

"How's your father? Still preaching the Gospel I hope."

"Yes, sir."

"Please tell him hello for me."

"I will, sir."

"Tim, one more thing. I would appreciate if this matter could be kept confidential."

"You have my strictest confidence and my prayers, sir. But I was just wondering, well, actually, more like hoping that you could shed some light on all of this for me."

"I'm not sure I know what you mean, Tim."

"She's not the same girl I remember from my childhood. I realize that people change, but this kind of change is just . . . too drastic. No one goes from being the way Bella was to the way she is now without some sort of traumatic incident happening." The Reverend frowned slightly at Tim, a patronizing gleam in his eyes, "There's been no incident, son. Tim, have you ever heard the saying: 'the devil always comes for the preacher man's child?' The greater the influence, the greater the impact you make against the kingdom of darkness, the harder the enemy comes after your seed. Bella is my only living heir, what better way for the enemy to try and get me to back down from the cause of Christ then to take my daughter's soul. But I will never back down, even if that means that my daughter will rot in hell." Tim blinked hard allowing LeBlanc's words to register.

"That's a hard truth for you to hear. I can tell. It's an even harder one for me to have to bear. Your father had to deal with the same thing when the devil tried to kill you with cancer. But yet I see you here before me today. Healed and totally cancer free, I assume?" "Yeah, totally free. Thanks to God inside Bella. The doctors had given up all hope for me. And frankly, so had my father, but your daughter laid hands on me, and I was healed. Sir, it pains me to say this, but it sounds to me like you have given up on Bella's healing. I know this must be tough for you and your wife. I can't imagine what this must have been like to watch such a shining star like Bella fall. But I am living proof that God can restore, and I will not stop praying until Bella is free."

Reverend LeBlanc cleared his throat and stood up. "Well, I don't mean to rush you, Timmy, but I do have revival tonight. We appreciate your confidence and your prayers."

CHAPTER 19

From her perch in the window seat, Sylvia watched Tim O'Brien walk back to his police cruiser and drive away. Thank God for small miracles. Tim was from a good church family in New Orleans. They could trust that he would keep his mouth shut about Bella. Sylvia sighed. She got up and walked into Bella's closet. At the very back she found what she was looking for, a modest floral print dress she had purchased last summer with the tags still on it. She placed the dress on the bed and selected a pair of shoes, new, and clean underwear, also new, for her daughter as well. And because she couldn't find one decent pair of pantyhose in Bella's drawer, Sylvia went down the hall to her own closet to retrieve a pair.

ꝏ

Bella sat in the bathtub soaking, Timmy's words running through her mind like the refrain of a song that couldn't be forgotten. *You were my Joshua. You walked me into the promised land of my healing.* Yes. She did remember praying for Tim that day. She remembered power going out from her hands, but had never known the results, that her simple act of childish faith had healed him.

"Guess you do come through sometimes for some people," Bella spoke grudgingly aloud to seemingly no one but the walls. "Thanks for Timmy. I liked him a lot, but what about me? Where's my Joshua at, God? Huh? What about me? "

ꝏ

Sylvia stood outside the bathroom door, clutching the package of pantyhose, listening intently to her daughter's sobs. *Lord, please this time let the tears mean that she's ready to repent.* Minutes later, Bella came out of the bathroom, freshly washed hair, glistening skin scrubbed so clean it was pink. Pink like the day Sylvia had brought her home from the hospital, so innocent, so pure, just her daughter, just her baby girl then. This picture perfect image of her daughter begged Sylvia to rewrite their history, coerced her to forget. With Bella

standing before her bathed, robed, and slippered, the stench of the sewer now completely gone, Sylvia could pretend that the LeBlancs where happy. Bella had not been missing for the last two weeks; she had been away at college. Actually it was missions—missions was the official story they had concocted for the congregation. Right after graduation, Bella had decided to take a year off from college, travel the world and do missions, while she sought the will of God for her life.

Everybody in New Orleans black churchdom, of course, knew this was a lie, but they got happy when the announcement went out across the pulpit anyway. Out of respect for their Pastor and First Lady, they let the lie ride. The LeBlancs were good god-fearing people. Wasn't their fault the devil came looking for their child.

But now, now, with her daughter standing before her looking so fresh and lovely, untainted by sin, and adorned in white, Sylvia could almost pretend that the existence she created for Bella was true. She could believe it and had. Until she noticed Bella staring at the respectable $1700 dress she had chosen for her with utter undisguised contempt. In that very instance, the spell was broken, the reality and the severity of the LeBlanc situation came crashing down around Sylvia like a house of glass. Sharp, jagged, colorful daggers hit her with so much force and so much clarity that Sylvia wanted to whip her daughter. To literally beat out whatever hell this was that had seeped its way into Bella's spirit. Sylvia was a heavy curser. She never cursed out loud because vulgar talk was not befitting a woman of her station. Sylvia only cussed in her mind. Right now, Sylvia's mind was cursing her daughter out for ruining a perfectly good fantasy and her picture prefect life.

Bella eyed the dress laying on the bed. "What?"

"You're going to the revival tonight. Tonight, just happens to be the last night, and I'm asking God to do a miracle for you. A suddenly. I need God to move, because this is not the way I raised you to be."

"Yeah, well whatever, but I'm not wearing that."

Sylvia bit her tongue hard to keep the cuss words inside. "You will wear it, and you will like it. If you don't like it, you will pretend like you do. You will march your high yellow behind up to that altar, and you will cry out to God. And we will put this whole awful mess behind us. Under the blood, where it belongs."

CHAPTER 20

As the praise and worship leader sang, Sylvia stood in the back of the church and watched her daughter. She had asked God for a miracle, but nothing like the sort of miracle she thought should be happening was. Everyone else at the altar rocked and cried out to God fervently to save them, to deliver them. Bella stood there unfazed, unmoved, looking like she had better things to do and people to see. Just when Sylvia was about to give up all hope, when it looked as if every prayer she had ever uttered on her daughter's behalf had been in vain, she noticed something else. The young, famous or rather infamous basketball player, Joshua Keys, who had been coming to the revival all week, the one who had re-dedicated his life to the Lord. He was looking at Bella, and Sylvia could tell it was more than mere curiosity. The young man was smitten. *Lord, could this be it, Bella's ram in the bush?* Sylvia slipped out of the sanctuary. She knocked once before entering her husband's office. Reverend Lamech LeBlanc sat at his desk, head bent over his Bible. He only looked up when he heard his wife approach.

"Bella at the altar?"

"Looking like she'd rather be anyplace else but there."

He took his glasses off and rubbed his eyes with his hands. "That girl's gonna be the death of me, Sylvia."

Sylvia stood behind his desk. With firm but gentle pressure she tried to rub the despondency from his shoulders. "Don't give up just yet. I got a feeling that things are about to turn around for Bella."

"What makes you say that?"

"Your newest protégée."

"Joshua?"

"I saw him looking at her. He likes her, Lamech. That boy's nose is wide open. Invite him to dinner tonight."

CHAPTER 21

Joshua studied the beautiful but withdrawn young woman seated across from him at the dinner table who had pretended to ignore him the entire night. This was, of course, a first for the handsome ball player, who never had to work to get a woman's attention a day in his life. Although he found her attitude curious, he was not in the least bit deterred. On the contrary, Joshua Keys loved a challenge.

He had been intrigued by her from the very first moment he'd picked her out of the crowd. She was at the altar. In a sea of wailing women, rolling on the floor, crying out to God, speaking in unknown tongues, Bella stood like a beautiful but wilted desert rose in a windstorm, totally unmoved by the gale of the spirit. She seemed to be waiting for something authentic to happen, and since nothing was happening—at least not for her, she felt no inclination to manufacture or to conjure. From his VIP position in the front of the church, Joshua could see that Bella's nonchalance was the source of much consternation on the part of her parents. And although he had come to respect and even revere the reverend, there was something about her quiet resistance to the status quo that made Joshua smile. If nothing else this girl was authentic. And Joshua valued realness and authenticity above all else. He was considering all of this when he heard the most peculiar thing–the quiet still voice of the Father, tell him to marry this woman, to take her as his bride.

"Your mom tells me you've been away doing missions work," Joshua said, attempting to engage the beautiful, distant girl in conversation once again. Her response was a snort that became a snicker that mounted into a giggle that became a full-blown riotous laugh. Mrs. LeBlanc blushed deeply, and the reverend choked on his water.

"Time for dessert. Bella. Help. Kitchen. *Now please*." Bella jumped up from the table and followed her mother into the kitchen like a petulant child.

"Now you listen here, Bella Rose, and you listen good," Sylvia said as she pulled her raspberry tart out of the oven and placed it on the counter. "That boy likes you. He's too naive of a Christian to see what you really are, so don't you dare mess this up.

Joshua Keys is your ram in the bush. Now you go back in there and act like you got some sense."

*

When the food was consumed, and the polite conversation had run its course, Joshua prepared to take his leave. "Mrs. LeBlanc, thank you, very much for inviting me to your home."

"You are most welcome. I hope you enjoyed my cooking enough to become a regular presence at our dinner table?" Sylvia gushed. Bella rolled her eyes.

Joshua smiled. "I did. I enjoyed your cooking immensely, but whether I come back or not, that depends entirely on Bella." He fixed his gaze on the girl then. As he had predicted, her big brown eyes meet his with a questioning stare. "Take a walk with me?"

Mrs. LeBlanc, clapped her hands in delight. "I think that's a wonderful idea. Lamech, don't you?"

Reverend LeBlanc nodded. "Joshua, knock on the door to my study when the two of you return."

CHAPTER 22

Bella followed Joshua outside but didn't go any further than the front steps. He reached out his hand to help her, but Bella folded her arms across her chest and glared down at him. "What you doing here, Bad Boy Joshua Keys, and what in the world could you possibly want with me?"

"I told you. I wanna take a walk."

Bella studied him for a moment before slowly descending the stairs behind him. They walked for a few minutes in silence.

"You must be a fan if you watch me play."

"I'm a fan of the game but not necessarily *your* game."

His smile was self-assured. Much too confident, Bella thought. Somebody needed to come along and take this brother down a few pegs.

"I'm the best baller in the NBA. What's not to like?"

"You fight too much. You should play the game more and stop letting it play you."

His eyes held a hint of a spark, but nothing like the over-the-top emotion Bella had witnessed him display on the court. "Sounds like the pot calling the kettle black."

"What's that supposed to mean?"

"It means you should take your own advice. I can see that you're a fighter too, but you don't have to be so adversarial with your parents all the time."

Bella stopped in her tracks. "You've been here for what, five minutes, and you think you have the right to judge me? You don't know them, you sure as hell don't know me."

She turned abruptly, stalked back in the direction of the LeBlanc home, muttering curses all the way.

"I know you better than you think," Joshua called after her. "I know that to be such an amazingly pretty girl you have a trash can for a mouth. I've seen ball players with mouths cleaner than yours. I know that you work overtime trying to be the opposite of what people expect you to be and that you can dish out truth, but you're much too fragile to handle hearing any of it yourself."

Bella marched back over to him. She pointed her finger in his face, well . . . technically his chest. At

6 feet 6 inches Joshua towered over her 5 foot 2 inch frame; all she could really reach was his chest.

"No, see, that's where you're wrong, cause ain't nothin' weak about me."

Joshua shrugged. "Prove it. Stay here and fight with me."

"Why should I?"

"You want to know my intentions towards you? You want to know if I'm looking for something real or if I just—"

"Wanna bone," Bella said flatly.

His dark eyes stared unflinchingly into hers. "You shouldn't believe everything you read in the funny papers, shorty."

"Oh, so Bad Boy Joshua Keys doesn't like to bone? And all those women throwing their panties on the court for you night after night, what a shame."

Bella watched his face for a reaction. No shame at all. Not even a little bit. *Humpf, here this joker was professing to be a Christian, and he didn't even have the good sense to be embarrassed.*

"Why are you laughing?" Bella demanded.

"Cause you make a whole lot of assumptions, shorty. I never said I didn't like it."

"What are you saying?"

"That I have the greatest respect for your father, and that same respect extends to you. You can relax, Bella Rose, at the moment, my intentions are completely honorable. Somebody told me something. I'd like to see for myself if it's true."

"Somebody told you something about me?

"Yeah."

She sucked her teeth. "Look who's reading the funny papers now?"

"You see, that's the thing, this particular person has never steered me wrong about anything before. Not ever. They never lie."

"Who's your infallible source?"

"God," Joshua answered evenly.

Bella blinked. "What do you think you hear?"

"That you're the other part of me. That I'm supposed to marry you, make you my wife."

Tim's words, the refrain of a song, flashed across Bella's mind like lightening. *You were my Joshua, Bella. You led me into the promised land of my healing.*

And so did her own question. *What about me?* For a fleeting moment, hope glistened in Bella's eyes, but she shook her head clearing her mind and eyes of fairy tales and dancing sugar plums. Then the hardness returned.

"That whole Cosby scene back there, don't believe the hype."

"Yeah your moms laid it on kind of thick, but I'm use to people trying to impress me."

"If you knew the truth, you'd run for the hills."

"Maybe. Maybe not."

"She lied. I don't do missions. I've been in the missionary position a whole bunch of times, but I ain't no missionary."

Bella waited for the shock and disgust to register on his face. Instead, she felt her heart take a nosedive off a cliff, when the corners of that beautiful mouth of his turned up into a crooked smile.

"Is that your colorful way of telling me that you like to bone?"

"You still think God tellin' you to marry me?"

Her pain was evident. She couldn't hide it, even if she tried. So she studied the sidewalk, their feet, the lamppost they had stopped under to have this conversation, anything and everything, but his eyes.

Joshua touched her then. With two amazingly smooth fingers he took his time and traced the contours of her face. His fingers trailed along her nose, her lips, they strummed across her cheekbones causing the color to rise to the surface of her skin. Joshua rested his fingers gently on the base of her chin and lifted her head to meet his eyes. "Is that your past?"

"Yes," she said, quietly, decisively, as if in that precise moment she was turning over a new leaf, becoming a whole a new person.

"Then I think I'd like to be a part of your future."

CHAPTER 23

Joshua wrapped lightly on Reverend LeBlanc's office door. "Joshua, come in, have a seat. How was your walk?" Joshua paused for a moment thinking of the best way to answer this question.

"It was colorful, sir."

The reverend nodded his head knowingly. Though Joshua suspected the older man couldn't possibly begin to grasp his meaning. "Sir, I'd like to ask permission to court, Bella." Reverend LeBlanc pretended to consider this.

"Have you consulted the Lord?"

"I have."

"Tell me, Joshua, what do you sense God saying?" Joshua shifted forward in his seat, realizing that he'd have to lay all his cards out on the table with the reverend same way he'd done with Bella tonight.

"I want you to know that you can speak freely with me, son."

"I know this may sound strange, and I assure you, I have never made this assertion about any other woman before, but I believe that God has told me that Bella is to be my wife." The minister sat back in his seat and studied Joshua for a beat.

"Why wait? Why bother with a courtship when you could step out in faith and do something extraordinary. Marry my daughter, take Bella as your bride."

"You'd entrust her to me, without fully knowing me?"

"I see the way you look at my daughter, Joshua. I saw tonight the way she looked at you, all the while pretending not to. There is biblical precedent for this. The Bible tells us that when Isaac saw Rebekah he loved her immediately. One week ago, when you walked up to that altar and recommitted your life to the Lord, God pointed you out to me and called you my son. I thought he was merely identifying my spiritual successor but this is so much better. This is the answer to many prayers. I'd marry you right here and now, if you were so inclined to."

Joshua shook his head. "I appreciate the prophetic significance of Isaac and Rebekah, but with all due respect, Rev, these ain't the Bible days. I don't want an arranged marriage any more than Bella does. When I ask her for her hand, she will say yes because I will have handled my business and won her heart." Joshua sat back in his chair and grinned over at Reverend LeBlanc. "Besides, I'm almost certain she wouldn't have me yet, and I'd never make a lifelong commitment without discussing it with my folks first."

"Of course, I understand, and you're right. Bella would hate the idea of any sort of arrangement. It amazes me that after spending such a short amount of time with her, you already know her so well. Joshua, I do feel led to caution you, because I sense that you and Bella's courtship will take the world by storm. It will be very quick. Don't expect people to understand. This is a faith move and people rarely understand moves of faith. God called Abraham and told him to get up and move to a land that he would show him, a land that his father and the rest of his kinsmen had never seen. Nobody understood that, and no one will understand your decision to marry Bella either. I tell you this, son, so that you won't be disappointed in your adopted family when they don't receive the news of your engagement well."

"My family loves me. They only want what's best for me. In time they'll see what I see, that Bella is God's best."

CHAPTER 24

When Jack and Melissa Kennedy got the call from their son Joshua telling them that he'd recommitted his life to Christ, had joined Reverend LeBlanc's church, and that he would marry LeBlanc's daughter, they dropped everything, left the ranch in the care of hired hands and made it to New Orleans on the next thing smoking. Melissa, for one, was happy about her son's recommitment to the Lord, yes. It had been a long time coming, and the answer to many prayers, but she had seen the mega pastor on television and she couldn't discern whether he was pushing snake oil or the real thing. This troubled her, and she didn't feel comfortable with Joshua sitting under a man like LeBlanc. And marrying a girl that Joshua hardly even knew, pastor's daughter or not, well that was completely out of the question.

She would do everything in her power to try and talk her son out of this foolishness. The Kennedys were taken on a whirlwind tour of LeBlanc's church.

They listened to LeBlanc explain the ends and outs of his ministry. How he believed himself to be a spiritual father to their son Joshua. How he believed that Joshua would one day preach the Gospel, and that when he was ready, he would take LeBlanc's mantle, and do it from his pulpit. They heard all about how LeBlanc likened himself to Moses, and how their Joshua was his Joshua, and he would lead his ministry into the promised land. They had driven to LeBlanc's grand home; met Sylvia LeBlanc, his wife. Joshua had proudly introduced them to their stunningly beautiful but shy daughter, Bella. Still, after all the glitter and all the gold, Jack and Melissa Kennedy were not convinced.

They'd just sat down to dinner in the LeBlanc's massive dining room when the proverbial shoe dropped. "We've booked the church for tomorrow afternoon at three," Sylvia said. "Joshua wanted to do the ceremony while his family was in town." Jack and Melissa both stared at each other. Joshua who sat across from them at the dinner table carefully measured their responses.

"I know this is a lot to take in at once, but this is the direction I've felt led to go," Joshua said, his voice strong and calm.

Jack spoke first. "You bet it's a whole lot to swallow, Joshie. You're just starting your career. I don't understand, why can't this wait?"

"I agree with your dad, honey. If Bell is really the one for you why can't the two of you wait?"

"Bella. Her name's Bella Rose," Sylvia corrected.

Melissa's cheeks colored. "Bella Rose, so sorry. Please, forgive me."

Jack leaned forward in his chair and addressed, Bella, who was sitting across the table beside Joshua. "Now, darling, don't you go taking that the wrong way. My wife didn't mean any disrespect. My Mel, is one of the kindest people you'll ever meet. It's just that our son has introduced you less than five minutes ago. He's getting married tomorrow, and here we haven't even got a chance to properly learn your name!"

"Dad, relax."

Reverend LeBlanc cleared his throat. He pulled an envelope out of the inside pocket of his dinner jacket. "We anticipated your feeling this way. To put your minds at ease, Sylvia and I had our attorney draw up a prenuptial agreement, which Bella will sign. We don't believe in divorce, but were things not to work out between Bella and Joshua, our daughter would return here with only what she brought into the relationship and my wife and I would continue to care for Bella, same as we always have."

Joshua shook his head. "No, no, pre-nup."

"Joshie!" Melissa cried.

"Mom, when Bella and I do this, we do it right."

"Are you sure about this, son?" Jack asked.

"I've never been more sure about anything in my life."

Jack ran a hand through his golden hair. "Son, if you insist on marrying, you know we'll support you."

"That's all I ask."

"Joshua, honey, I want to support you. I really do. I just don't understand this at all."

"Mom," Joshua said softly, speaking to the fear he saw spreading across her clear blue eyes. "You've always encouraged me to respond to His leading."

"But Joshie, why would God tell you to marry a girl you hardly even know, yolk yourself to these people you don't even know."

Reverend LeBlanc bristled. "These people? Now we're these people."

"Lamech, honey, calm down," Sylvia said.

"Mrs. Kennedy, have you looked at your son's skin lately? We are his people."

"You're taking her words out of context, this has nothing to do with skin color!" Jack said.

"You're his people because you're black?" Melissa shot back.

"Yes, because we're black. Black people in this country share a commonality that you'll never understand. Perhaps you think this is some ploy to get Joshua's money. Well, let me assure you, Mrs. Kennedy, my coffers are full. Whether Bella marries your son or not, she will always be financially taken care of. This is about the will of God being performed in your son's life."

"So you know the will of God for my son's life, and for your daughter's life for that matter?"

"I believe in pre-destiny. I believe that before God formed Bella in my wife's womb and before he formed Joshua in his natural mother's womb, he ordained this union to be."

"You mean his black mother don't you?" Melissa jumped up from the table, upsetting her chair in the process.

"Mom, please sit down," Joshua said.

Jack rose quickly and resettled Melissa's chair. "Mel, darling, I think you'd better calm down."

"No, Jack. I will not calm down! Don't you hear what he is saying? I'm no pastor, Mr. LeBlanc, but I know a little bit about pre-destiny myself. I know that before Joshua was formed in his black mother's womb he was predestined to be mine. My son Michael also. God gave them to me. And when he did, he didn't care that my skin was white!"

"Oh, this is preposterous!" Reverend LeBlanc fumed. "What could you possibly have to offer! You can never understand what it's like to be a black man coming of age in America."

Jack was suddenly at LeBlanc's side. "Now, you just hold on a second, buddy. What the hell are you saying?"

"I think I just made myself perfectly clear."

"Yeah, you did. I think we better step outside."

Reverend LeBlanc stood up from the table. "Alright, let's go."

Sylvia gasped, "Lamech!"

Joshua's hand came down hard on the dining room table. "Enough!" He glared at the two men. "I can't believe this. So now what? The two of you gon go outside and fight. Then what?"

The room fell silent. Jack and Lamech glowered at each other. Joshua pushed away from the table. "You know what? Have at it. Beat the hell out of each other. I'm out. " Joshua looked down at Bella. "You coming or what?"

Bella jumped up from her seat at the dining room table and scurried after him.

"Joshua, wait!" Jack called at his back. Jack followed Joshua and Bella out of the house. "Son, we need to talk about this."

Joshua opened the passenger side for Bella. He jumped into his convertible and without a backwards glance sped off.

"Don't do anything stupid!" Jack called as the car peeled away from the curb.

CHAPTER 25

The Kennedys and the LeBlancs sat across from each other in the parlor wordlessly watching the clock, waiting for their children's return. When the doorbell chimed, both couples bolted for the front door. A few courteous introductions were made and the LeBlanc's walked back into the parlor crestfallen as Melissa flew into her oldest son's arms. Mike looked down at his mother's tear-streaked face, then over at his father for an explanation.

"Things got a little heated between the Reverend and me. Your brother got pissed, he stormed out of here nearly an hour ago with Bella."

"Jack, how could we behave so foolishly? I will never forgive myself if he runs off and marries without our blessing."

Mike wrapped his arms around Melissa. "You know he won't do that. He just needs to cool down a bit. He'll come back when he's ready. In the meantime, you two need to go back in there and smooth things over with the LeBlancs."

❧

Two hours later a car pulled up out front. Reverend LeBlanc went to the window to investigate. "That's them," he said. Both couples stood and started for the door.

"Stop."

Both sets of parents turned to see Mike still seated. "Seriously people, you really don't want to crowd him right now."

Reverend LeBlanc held his hands up in surrender. "Okay, Michael, how do you suggest we proceed?"

"For starters, since I'm not the one who pissed him off let me talk to him first." Mike looked sternly at the four pair of eyes now trained on him. "When they come inside, don't say a word, listen."

"We'll follow your lead. You know him best, Mikey," Jack said.

Reverend LeBlanc nodded solemnly. "That does appear to be the wisest course of action."

Mike walked out of the house, just as Bella and Joshua were getting out the car. Joshua let out a shout of exaltation upon seeing his brother, and Mike pulled Joshua into a crushing bear hug. Mike finally released his brother and looked him over carefully, "I got here a few hours ago. I heard what happened. You straight?"

"I'm good, just needed get my head on right. I'm glad you made it."

"Please, bro, you know I wouldn't miss this for the world."

"Mike, this is my fiancé, Bella Rose LeBlanc. Bella, this is my older brother, Michael Dutton."

Bella stuck her hand out toward Mike. "I know who he is. It's a pleasure to finally meet you. I'm a real fan of your game."

Joshua frowned down at Bella. "Oh, so now you a fan?"

Bella shrugged. "What can I say, he plays the game, it doesn't play him."

"She's smart, Josh. I like this girl."

"More like a smart aleck," Joshua said, as he playfully popped Bella on the behind.

"Pleasure's all mine, Bella, but in this family we do hugs not handshakes." Mike opened his long arms and Bella stepped into them for a hug. Mike lowered his 6'7" frame and whispered into Bella's ear, "I've been telling my brother that same thing for years."

"Bella, go inside, let me talk to my brother for a minute, alright?" Joshua said.

"Okay."

The two men leaned up against Joshua's car and watched Bella walk up the stairs into the house.

"Baby girl's fine, Josh."

"Yeah."

"But Mom and Dad do have a point. You just met this girl, something could be seriously wrong. You gotta ask yourself why would her parents agree to this so quickly? Mom and Dad asked me to come out here and talk you out of this. I know how stubborn you get when you've made your mind up about something, so I won't even try that approach. But as your brother, I do need to make sure that before you walk down that aisle tomorrow, you're completely sure about this."

"Member the story mom used to tell about when you came to live with us? I was two and you were five. How the first time you saw me, you declared to everyone who would listen, that I was your baby brother."

"I remember."

"We been brothers ever since, right?"

"Fo life."

Joshua pointed towards the sky. "I heard Him tell me that she was my bride. She's not perfect, man. I already see that. But she's mine, and I've never been this sure about anything in my life. "

"That's good enough for me. Let's get you married."

CHAPTER 26

When Joshua and Bella walked into the parlor, the Kennedys and LeBlancs did just as Mike had suggested, they remained seated and silent. Joshua stood in front of them holding Bella's hand. Mike stood behind him leaning up against the wall. Joshua surveyed the two older couples seated before him.

"Let me tell you how this is going to go down. Bella and I will be married tomorrow in a private ceremony at the LeBlanc's church. Pastor Dobbs will fly in to perform the wedding." Joshua looked at Melissa. "I asked him not to say anything to you or Dad until we had announced our engagement, but Bella and I have been meeting with him privately for over a month." A look of surprised relief flew across Melissa's face.

"He's known you practically your whole life. I'm very glad you sought his spiritual counsel, before you decided to marry." Melissa shot a furtive glance over at Reverend LeBlanc, making sure her words had not offended.

Joshua's mouth turned up into a half smile. "Of course I sought his counsel. I'm just in love, Mom, I haven't completely lost my ability to reason. I realize now that I should have let you in on what I was thinking way before now. That way I could have prepared you better for this." Joshua pulled Bella in front of him and wrapped her protectively in his arms. "After I calmed down enough to listen to reason, Bella helped me to see your side of things. So I apologize for that."

Melissa smiled gratefully at Bella who smiled back. "Thank you," Melissa said softly.

"I need you to understand that this is my decision, not the Rev's. Nobody's been brainwashed here."

Jack nodded. "Of course not, Joshie. We know you better than that."

Joshua looked pointedly at his mother.

"The four of us got a chance to talk while you two were out, and I do understand that as well." Melissa said quietly.

Joshua shifted his hard gaze to Reverend LeBlanc. "I need you to respect my parents, Rev, I need you to honor the unique position that each person in this room holds in my life."

"Joshua, I apologize. My behavior this afternoon was shameful. You have my word, this will never happen again."

CHAPTER 27

Bella stood on a wooden box while her mother tucked and pinned her dress. "This is God's providence, Bella Rose. This is your chance to turn your life around. Now you only get one so use it wisely." Sylvia stood up. She fluffed the veil to her daughter's brazenly white wedding dress and sighed contently, examining her handiwork. "Those days as a Mary Kay consultant really paid off. You look fabulous if I do say so myself." Sylvia studied her daughter's face. Bella looked like a race horse at the starting gate ready to bolt. "Oh, baby, are you nervous? If you're worried about love, that'll come later. That's how it was with your daddy and me. Please don't worry about that."

Bella shook her head. "It's not that, Mama. I don't want to do this here."

"Oh, Bella, please don't cry! You'll ruin your make up." Sylvia fanned her daughter's face until the tears in her eyes disappeared. "Now, Bella, after the stir you and Joshua created running out of the house yesterday, don't tell me that you've up and changed your mind?"

"Of course not, it's just . . . I thought I could do it, but I don't want to be getting ready to start over here. And I don't want him to walk me down the aisle on the happiest day of my life."

"Don't be disrespectful. This place is the house of God, and the him you are referring to, is your daddy. Now of course he's going to give you away. How would it look if he didn't? Your daddy loves you very much. He's paid a whole lot of people to keep quiet about you, Bella Rose. That's what love will do for you. Love covers a multitude of sins." Sylvia turned Bella around so she could see herself in the full length mirror. Bella blinked as if seeing herself for the first time. "See, I told you. You're absolutely stunning."

In the sanctuary the organist began to play. Bella managed a weak smile. "I guess that's my cue."

Sylvia nodded. She hesitated for a moment then called out at her daughter's departing back. "Bella?"

Bella turned around and faced her mother. "Yes, Mama?"

"When you go to your husband tonight pretend it's your first time. Cry a little bit, alright. For me. No good girl ever enjoys it on her first time."

August, 2005

CHAPTER 28

New Orleans, Monday Aug. 29, 2005, 3:00 AM

At three o'clock in the morning, a sense of panic swept over the city. One by one, eyes that had been deep in slumber popped open at the sound of the rain tumbling onto the rooftop like rocks, rocks that fell from the sky with the speed and intensity of a passing freight train. The residents who decided not to heed Mayor Nagin's request and leave the city stayed for various reasons. Some had stayed because New Orleans had been the city of their birth and they didn't have no other place to go. Others stayed cause they didn't have the transportation or the financial means to leave. And, then of course, there were those that had lived through Betsy and Camille. But at three o'clock that morning, with the rain sounding like thunder, every soul that remained in the city began to re-think their decision.

Maybe I should have called my sister in Detroit and asked her to send me a little money. Maybe I should've gotten a ride with a neighbor. I could have asked for an advance on my check, got a ride with a co-worker, a friend, hell the friend of a friend. I could have offered them a few dollars for gas.

Marcus laid in bed listening to the sound of the rain and thinking about a video his science teacher had showed in class called *Hurricanes*. They hadn't seen the worst of it yet. They hadn't seen wind velocities that could snap a tree like a tooth pick. No, this sound that sounded like a drive-by outside his front door, this wasn't the storm. This was the opening act before the concert. And something told Marcus that the real storm would be a killer. Marcus jumped up, grabbed his jeans, a hoodie and his Timberlands. An umbrella in this weather would be pointless. He had been the man of the house ever since his granddad died when he was seven. If they were ever gonna make it out of New Orleans alive it would be up to him to make it happen.

CHAPTER 29

New Orleans, 6:00 A.M. Monday, Aug. 29, 2005

B*ella, Bella Rose, get up, take Jabari, and leave the city now. I can do nothing here, until you leave."*

Bella's eyes popped open with a start. She sat up in bed and looked around the room, momentarily disoriented. Looking for a bag to throw some things into she heard the voice again, crystal clear.

"Take nothing, go quickly, warn the others."

Bella felt herself being lifted up off the bed with a strength that was not her own. She put on the clothes she was sure she hadn't laid out for herself, and ran into Jabari's room. Jabari, usually a hard sleeper, who was nearly impossible to wake, awoke instantly when Bella called his name. He had fallen asleep in his clothes.

"Jabari, we have to leave, we gotta get out of here, right now!"

Bella and Jabari ran through the apartment complex screaming and banging on doors. One by one the remaining households of the Dunbar Street apartment complex awoke. It wasn't until she ran outside and looked around that Bella remembered the reason they were still stuck in there in the first place. Her car had been repossessed. *Alright God, what do I do now?* No sooner than the thought had been formulated, a yellow school bus pulled up in front of the building. The doors of the bus opened and the residents, who were huddled together under the porch's flimsy awning, let out a shout of victory as Marcus darted quickly from the bus.

"Thank you, Lord!" Pearl said as she grabbed her grandson and hugged him tightly. "I knew our help would come!"

"Listen up, people!" Walter Trendale said. He had to shout to be heard over the pounding rain, "We gotta make it to higher ground. At the rate this rain is falling I don't think those levees are gonna hold. We gotta go now! If this storm doesn't kill us, the flood waters will!"

"Is everybody accounted for?" Maggie Trendale asked.

"Charlie's not here!" said Lola Terry, his wife. "He said he ain't going nowhere, and Sally upstairs, stayed too."

"Oh, no!" Maggie cried. "She stayed? I thought for sure she left with her sons! Walter, Sally's confined to a wheelchair. She can't get out by herself!"

"Maggie, you and Rosemary get everybody on the bus! The boys and I will go get Sally. We'll carry her out."

"Don't forget Charlie!" Lola shouted at Walter's back. "He don't want to leave but somebody's gotta talk some sense into him!"

Bella and Maggie each hoisted one of Maggie and Walter's children up into their arms and made a mad dash for the bus. When they had gotten the two girls settled on the bus, they ran back for Pearl and Lola. Bella was going back up the stairs behind Lola when Charles Terry grabbed her by the leg.

"Where do you think you're going, Rosemary?"

Bella struggled to free herself, but the hand on her ankle felt like a vice grip. Terry dragged her off the bus, banging her head on the bottom step in the process.

"Everybody git! Git back in the building right now! Nobody's going nowhere! You hear me? Nowhere!"

The water was rising faster. It was up to Terry's ankles. Bella's head was underwater on the ground. She angled her body and lifted her torso up so she wouldn't drown. She clawed frantically at her neck for air and felt the clasp on the cheap gold chain give way, and the one hope she had left—her wedding ring float away from her.

Lola stood on the bottom stair of the school bus watching dumbfounded. "Charlie, let go of that gal. Can't you see, we gotta go?"

"Shut up, Lola, and git your fat hide off that bus!"

Maggie pushed her way past Lola and lunged onto Charlie's back. She clawed at his face, his neck. He knocked Maggie to the ground.

This is it, Bella thought. *This is how it ends for me. I'm going to drown in New Orleans, in four inches of water.* That's when Bella heard it again, the voice, crystal clear just like the last time.

"Be still, Bella, don't struggle. The Egyptians who pursue you today, you will never see them again."

Walter, Marcus, and Jabari appeared in the doorway. They lowered the older woman's wheelchair down, gently onto the porch, just for a moment to catch their breath. Walter looked up. He saw his wife on the ground, Lola Terry screaming like a loon, and the cause of it all—Charles Terry. The next thing Walter saw was red.

"Mom!" Jabari screamed. He lurched towards her. Walter held his arm out to block him. "Stay!" In one liquid motion Walter grabbed a bat leaning against the doorframe and flew towards Charles Terry.

"No! Walter, don't hurt him!" Lola screamed. Suddenly, thunder cracked open the sky. A bolt of lightning struck Terry in the chest. Walter smashed the bat down hard on Terry's hand, breaking the connection between him and Bella Rose just before the current was able to travel down his arm. The force of the impact knocked both Walter and Bella back several feet. Jabari ran to his mother. Bella covered her son's face in her skirt. For a moment, the pounding rain sounded like dull background music next to the popping, crackling, hissing sounds of frying flesh that filled the air. Bella watched Terry's eyeballs melt from their sockets. Still reaching for her, his lifelessly body jerked and sizzled on the ground.

Maggie screamed as she and Marcus ran towards Walter. "Walter your leg, it's bleeding bad!"

Walter looked down at the gaping hole in his trouser pants and smiled reassuringly up at his wife. "It's only a flesh wound, darling. Just give me something to stop the blood."

Maggie quickly tore the sleeve off her shirt, and Walter tied it around the wound.

Walter stood. "Let's get the hell outta here. Maggie, you and Matthew help Rose up onto the bus.

I think I might have broken her ankle. Marcus, you help me lift Ms. Sally."

Lola stood sobbing besides the still, charred remains of her husband. Pearl, who had been blocking the two youngest children's view of the situation, called to her from the safety of the bus.

"He gone now, Lola. God willed it, so ain't nothing you can do about it, cept keep living and get on this bus."

Slowly, Lola turned, she walked up the stairs, and took her seat. Sad for Charlie, but grateful to still be in the land of the living. He hadn't been a good husband. In fact, he had been downright hateful. Lola cried anyhow, because he was the only husband she'd ever known, and because even a dog shouldn't have died like that.

CHAPTER 30

6:22 AM, New Orleans

They had driven one block when Marcus turned the corner and pulled up in front of an old abandoned warehouse. "Why, are we stopping?" Lola asked. "Are we out of gas?"

Marcus turned around and addressed the passengers on the bus. "Look, everybody, I'm gon get y'all out of here, I promise. But I gotta go get my mama. I can't leave her like this."

BOOM! A loud explosion rang out in the distance.

"Oh God! Armageddon is upon us! We gon die!" Lola screamed. "We all gon die!"

"Quiet!" Walter bellowed. "Now I think that sound means the levees just broke. That means these lower wards are going be the first to fill up. So that means you got five minutes, Marcus. Five minutes, you hear me? And no more. Then we have to leave, alright? With or without her."

Marcus nodded and quickly sprinted from the bus. Three excruciatingly long minutes later, Marcus came out of the crack house with a kicking, screaming Belinda in tow.

She had been smoking her crack pipe when he found her, having just recently discovered someone's abandoned stash. To her dismay, Marcus had burst into the building, tossed her pipe and her new found stash without even so much as a word. He scooped her up like a sack of potatoes and threw her over his back. Belinda was cursing him furiously, biting and clawing at his face and neck. When they got to the bus Belinda planted both feet firmly on the sides of the doorway and arched her body backwards.

Walter got off and helped Marcus wrestle Belinda the rest of the way up onto the bus. Belinda was still cursing and flailing when Walter Trendale slammed her body down onto the seat. Belinda jumped back up, ready to attack again. Suddenly Pearl was up on her feet. She slapped Belinda hard across the face, shocking the crazed woman back into her seat.

"Sit down. Don't you get back up, don't you say another word. So help me God, I will knock you into next week!"

Marcus took his place in the driver's seat, his chest rising and falling in quick time from the struggle with Belinda. He swatted at the long red scratches on his face and neck as he stared at Jabari. "I can get us over the bridge into Texas, when we get there you think your pops can help us?"

Jabari nodded. "For sure."

CHAPTER 31

Houston, Texas, 9 AM

Joshua awoke to the sound of his alarm clock. He had fallen asleep on his knees in the prayer position. In his partially awakened state, Joshua heard the voice on the radio say something about a category five hurricane hitting Louisiana and the surrounding gulf cities. Then the voice said something that forced him completely awake. "New Orleans as we know it is gone."

CHAPTER 32

Maggie sat back down on the seat next to Bella in the very back of the bus. "I'm afraid she not looking no better." They had been on the road now for about an hour. Twice Maggie had gotten up to check on Ms. Sally. Maggie's two girls had managed to sleep, thankfully, so had the distraught Lola Terry. Belinda, who was coming down from her high, was stone cold knocked out. It was a good thing too, because Pearl sat directly beside her ready to make good on her promise.

"I just wish we had something to give her," Maggie said.

Bella patted her friend's hand. "We'll be in Texas soon. We'll find help there. I know we will."

"Lord, Texas. I don't know what we gonna do. Least ya'll got someplace to go."

Bella shook her head. "My son has someplace to go. I'm in the same boat as everybody else. But knowing Joshua will do right by him that's good enough for me."

"The other night when Walter was on the phone he said Joshua called you Bella and he called Matthew Jaban or something."

Bella sighed. "Jabari. When we came to New Orleans five years ago we assumed new identities so that Joshua wouldn't find us. I'm sorry I didn't tell you, Maggie. Truthfully, I didn't plan on us becoming such good friends. "

"You never cease to amaze me, Rose. All this time I've been thinking you broke like the rest of us, and here all along you high society."

"Joshua is the rich one. Not me."

"Y'all still married, right?"

"For the time being."

"So, you left because he was hitting you?"

"No. Maggie, I know what the media has put out there about Joshua, but he's really not a violent person at all. He's never been abusive to me or Jabari, not physically, verbally, or otherwise."

"So explain to me why you vacationing in the ghetto when you got a rich, handsome, husband who ain't beating you, waiting at home?"

"He's not waiting for me, Maggie. Joshua doesn't love me anymore."

Sudden unbidden tears rushed to the surface. The tears were a surprise to both Bella and Maggie, who looked around for tissue. Of course there was no tissue to be found. The best Maggie could offer was a shoulder to cry on. Bella lowered her voice, on the off chance that Jabari might hear her, even though Jabari was busy holding visual with Walter and Marcus at the very front of the bus.

"I don't blame him. I messed up my marriage a long time ago, Maggie. I did things that were unforgiveable. Jabari is . . . Jabari is not Josh's, blood child. After we came to Texas, I had an affair."

"Does Joshua know?" Maggie asked, as gently as possible.

"He knew, he adopted Jabari, gave him his name on the day he was born. But he never fully forgave me. He was so angry and hurt. He started getting into even more fights on and off the basketball court. Then the paternity suits came. None of them ever panned out to be worth the paper they were printed on, but I had brought home a baby by another man, so what could I say? He was such a good man when I met him, and I knew I was ruining him. So I left."

"He sent the private eye to find you, that's gotta count for something. Why would he go through all that trouble and expense, if he didn't love you?

Especially if," and Maggie lowered her voice as well, just in case someone else on the bus was listening, "Jabari is not his biological child. If that's not love, honey, I don't know what is."

"He sent the private eye," Bella said flatly. "That's how I know."

"What?"

"He always comes for me himself. He sent somebody else this time, that's how I know he's done with me."

"Rose, what do you mean, always? You mean you've run away like this before?"

"It's a long story, Maggie, but the short answer is, yes."

"Well, it ain't like I got any chores to do, seeing as how everything I own just been swept away in a hurricane. Ain't got nothing but time. So you can go on and give me the long version."

So Bella told her the story of her life. She spoke words she hadn't breathed to another living soul. "I came out here to get a new life, cause outside of Joshua, New Orleans was the only thing I'd ever known. I figured since this was the place where I died, that this should be the place of my rebirth. I wanted to prove to myself that I could make it in this world without a man. And when I finally got myself together, then I'd come back to him, but now that he sent the divorce papers, I know that will never happen."

Maggie sat back in her seat. "Wow, I don't know what to say. I guess my first question is, what do I call you now? "

Bella smiled at her friend. "Actually, you can call me what you been calling me, Rose. My given name is Bella Rose."

"Well, nice to meet you, Bella Rose." Maggie smiled wryly and reached out her hand in greeting.

"Well, I heard everything you just said, and I think that maybe Joshua Keys has had a change of heart. You know we watch a lot of basketball in our house. My husband just happens to be your husband's biggest fan. According to the media, he's not Bad Boy Joshua Keys anymore. He found the Lord."

Bella scoffed. "You'll excuse me if I don't put too much stock in that. Every Christian I've ever met has been nothing but a hypocrite."

"Oh really now, so where does that leave me?"

Bella wrinkled her nose in disgust. "You're not really a Christian are you?"

"Yes, Rose, I am."

"Well, you're different."

"Different my foot. Rose, I just heard your life story. You came to Christ, all by yourself, walked up to the altar, when you were five years old. You led a revival at youth camp and everybody got saved."

Bella shook her head. "That was before. These days I don't know if I even believe He exists anymore. If God is so real, why didn't He protect me?"

"You're angry cause of what you went through, Rose. That's normal and to be expected. I don't know why things happen to so many of us when we are children. I don't know why He didn't stop your daddy. But He sent you Joshua, and He sent Walter to me. The children of Israel was in slavery for 400 years, and God sent them Moses. Lord knows they went through something awful, but that didn't mean God didn't love them, in fact, He said He chose them."

Bella thought about this for a moment and remembered Maggie's pain. She couldn't necessarily relate to the children of Israel, but she could relate to Maggie. Maggie had shared with Bella about a brutal rape she'd suffered as a child. And here she was today with no bitterness towards the men who raped her. Somehow she could be and live in the world with peace.

"God's not so bad. He got us out of New Orleans today," Maggie said, pulling Bella away from her thoughts. "When I think about that mean old Charles Terry getting struck down like that, how you could have died, how Walter could have died. You gotta see that was the hand of God, Rose. Know what I think? I think prayer is like riding a bicycle. You never forget. In fact, I think you should pray right now."

"Me?"

"Yes, ma'am, you."

"I don't know what to say."

"Anything you want to say, Rose. All prayer is, is a conversation with God."

Bella looked out the window at the pouring rain. "God, let us make it out of this storm alive and please don't let nobody else die."

CHAPTER 33

Mike stood outside Joshua's house ringing the doorbell. When Joshua didn't answer, Mike walked around back, punched the key code in and entered the house through the garage. He walked past Joshua's H1 and Bella's Bugatti the one she left behind when she took Jabari and left five years ago. Something about her leaving the car this time had told Joshua that she was serious. That she didn't want to be found. Mike hadn't been in his brother's garage in a long time. He didn't even know that Joshua had held on to the car. The shine coming from the fender told him that it had been freshly detailed. Mike knew that Joshua had a guy that came by the house once a week to detail his truck, apparently the guy had been detailing Bella's car too. He knew his brother didn't drive it. He didn't even like to ride in it. It was a sports car made for a woman, Joshua had often complained.

"Josh!" Mike called as he entered the house. He heard the television; it was the CNN on the minute report of the Hurricane Katrina details. Mike took the stairs two at a time to the upstairs master bedroom. When he entered Josh's bedroom he found his brother laying on the bed staring up at the ceiling. The sound of the TV was loud from downstairs, but inside the master bedroom it was blaring. "Josh!" Still no answer. Mike picked up the remote and shut off the television. Joshua sat up in bed and looked over at Mike. "I've been calling you all morning, man. You alright?"

"Last night I saw their bodies floating on the water in my dream. You think God was trying to prepare me?"

Mike avoided looking directly into his brother's eyes, not because he believed his family was dead, but because he couldn't stand seeing the pain there. He walked into the master bedroom closet and returned a few minutes later with some clothes. "Get dressed, man, we gotta go."

"I already tried to get a plane. They ain't letting anybody in or out of the airspace over Louisiana for the next 24 hours."

"You got a press conference scheduled at Home Court in an hour. All the major stations will be there. You're going to make a statement to the press and we're going to post a reward. That PI you hired got any recent photos of them?"

"Yeah," Joshua said, suddenly thawing and coming back to life. He slipped on the slacks and was now buttoning the dress shirt that Mike had handed him. Joshua motioned to the large manila envelope sitting on the top of the dresser.

"Good, we're gonna need them." Mike grabbed a duffel bag from the closet and threw the pictures from the PI as well as some personal effects like Joshua's tooth brush, hair brush, and electric razor into the bag. Mike looked up from his packing and found Joshua staring down at the wing tipped shoes he had set in front of him.

"Josh, you ready?"

Joshua looked up at him, and Mike caught the pain that he had been trying to avoid seeing in his brother's eyes.

"Their apartment was in the heart of the city. Unless she got out, there's no way they could have survived. I just found them Mike, I—I can't lose them now. . . Not again."

Mike grabbed Joshua by the neck and pulled him into a quick embrace. "It ain't over, little brother, alright? It ain't over till God says it's over." The two men released each other and Mike scanned the room looking for any other items he had forgotten. He saw

Joshua's cell phone sitting on the charger on the dresser next to his truck keys. Mike grabbed the cell phone and the keys. He threw the cell phone to Joshua who caught it effortlessly, and the two men walked out the door.

"Let's take your truck," Mike said, leading the way out the house through the garage. "More room." Mike jumped in the driver's seat, adjusted the mirrors and backed the truck expertly out of the garage. "Some of the brothas are over at the church praying now. We'll stop by there for a few before we go to the office. I want you to have your head on straight when you meet the press."

CHAPTER 34

When they pulled up to the church, the parking lot was uncharacteristically full for a Monday. Joshua and Mike entered the sanctuary. There, about two hundred men, women, and children from the church had assembled themselves to pray for their newest assistant pastor. They huddled around Joshua and prayed passionately and earnestly, that God might give him favor, that he might find his family in the mist of this awful tragedy, and that until God worked a miracle on Joshua's behalf, He might give Joshua His peace that passes all understanding. Peace in the midst of the storm.

CHAPTER 35

10:18 A.M. Houston Texas, Astrodome

At exactly 10:18 A.M. Marcus arrived at the Astrodome. As far as the eye could see, there were police barricades and distraught relatives holding up signs and pictures of loved ones. The bus doors opened and camera crews and reporters from the various networks rushed the bus. Marcus quickly closed the doors. One reporter managed to get his arm through before the door closed. He pointed his microphone up towards Marcus, as he and the other reporters fired questions at them.

"How'd you get out of New Orleans alive?"

"You are Hurricane Katrina evacuees?"

"What was it like being in the midst of a category five hurricane like Katrina?"

"Did you fear for your lives?"

Maggie looked into Ms. Sally's now listless eyes. "Walter, we've got to get Ms. Sally some help." Walter looked over at the woman, going into diabetic shock. An ex-marine, he didn't fight all this way for nothing, certainly not to let somebody die on his watch. He stood on the steps of the bus and spoke to the reporters outside.

"Look, we've just been through hell and high water, literally, and after that, the ride of our lives. We got a sick woman on this bus who needs medical attention. We don't have time to be answering no questions. So back away from the dag gon bus!"

"Sir, you look like you've been wounded, did you receive your injury trying to escape Hurricane Katrina?" a reporter called from outside the bus.

Four health care professionals and two police officers ran out of the Astrodome. The police officers began to deal with the crowd of reporters that had flooded the bus while the team of health care workers stood on point with oxygen and a gurney, ready to receive any wounded who may be on the bus. Walter allowed the four health care workers onto the bus. They loaded up Ms. Sally and got her off first. Pearl and Belinda were the next to exit the bus, followed by Marcus, Lola, Maggie Trendale, Walter, and their two children. Bella and Jabari were the last to leave. The former Dunbar Street apartment residents were bombarded on every side by people holding signs and pictures asking, "Have you seen this woman?" or "Have you seen this little girl?" "Have you seen my nephew? He's just a baby, please, he's only two."

"No, I'm sorry, I'm sorry," Bella replied, over and over again, her heart aching every time she did. She had family in New Orleans too, but she couldn't think about that now. If she did, she might crumble. She hadn't spoken to her father in ten years, and the last conversation with her mother had been so awful—the thought of something happening to her mother made Bella suddenly weak at the knees. But then, thankfully, Maggie's hand was there on her shoulder maneuvering their little group past the depressing crowd.

"Come on, everyone, let's get inside."

They were family now, they'd weathered the storm together, that made them responsible for one another's lives. The group turned around and went back outside when they saw that their fearless leader was no longer with the pack.

"He must have gotten held up by a reporter," someone decided. But when they got outside, they all saw Walter walking away from the Astrodome.

"Walter, where are you going?" Maggie called

"I'll be back later, Maggie. I gotta find a job." The shirt sleeve that she'd tied around his leg earlier that morning to stop the bleeding, was now caked with black blood. One of the aid workers standing by looked at Walter. "Sir, you need medical attention. We need to look at that leg, at least let us bandage it correctly, so it doesn't get infected."

Walter shook his head. "Naw, man. I need to find a job so I can feed my family."

"Walter, please." Maggie begged. "There'll be plenty of time for that later, let's just wait awhile. Find out where we gonna be."

"We ain't gonna be nowhere if I don't find a job, woman. Now stop worrying and take the others back inside."

Marcus looked at Maggie. "He should take my cell phone, so that we can at least reach him.

"That's true," Bella said. "We might be able to borrow somebody else's phone to call him."

Lola spoke up. "Walter, wait. Take Charlie's phone. We'll call you on Marcus's phone if we need to get in touch with you." She handed him the cell phone. Maggie and her children hugged Walter tightly. The Dunbar Street residents stood watching until Walter disappeared completely out of sight. It wasn't until he got about a block away from the Astrodome when the thought occurred to him. *How in the world am I gonna get a job dressed like this?*

CHAPTER 36

Inside the Astrodome, a young brunette reporter respectfully approached Marcus for an interview. "Which one of these ladies is your mother?" The Dunbar Street women glared at her.

"We all his mama," Lola Terry said with her hands on her hips. "Who wants to know?"

"Well, I do. My name is Connie James, and I'm a reporter with CNN. I'm just looking for someone who is able to sign a release form for Marcus, saying he can talk to the press. I think that what Marcus has done, commandeering a school bus and driving his family out of New Orleans, is remarkable. I think the rest of the world should know about it. I'd like to be the one to tell his story."

"Any money in it?" Belinda asked.

Pearl cut her eyes at Belinda, silencing her with a look. "I'm Marcus's grandmother, Pearl Anderson. I'm his legal guardian, but Marcus is the man of the house. He can decide to talk to you if he wants to or not."

"It's okay Grandma, I don't mind," Marcus said. Connie's assistant held out a pen and the form attached to a clipboard. Pearl looked over the document suspiciously. Finally, after being reassured again by Connie that she was not signing away any of Marcus' legal rights, she signed her name. The Dunbar Street apartment women stood waiting, arms folded, feet tapping, for the reporter to ask her first question.

Marcus looked uneasily over at the women. "Uh, it's okay y'all. I can handle this. Why don't y'all go check on Ms. Sally." Marcus looked at Jabari, and gave him a knowing nod. "Find out where we gonna sleep tonight. I'll come find y'all when I'm finished here."

"Okay, Marcus, if that's what you want." Pearl said. Everyone turned to go, except Belinda. Belinda sucked her teeth. "I think I'm a stay here and make sure your rights don't get violated."

Marcus shot Pearl a pleading look. The older woman marched over to Belinda and grabbed her by the arm. "Let's go!"

The five women, Jabari, and the Trendale girls, made their way to the roped off section of the Astrodome that served as the makeshift hospital area.

The line for people checking into the Astrodome was so long it wound out the door.

"Somebody needs to stand in the line and get our stuff, it ain't getting no shorter," Maggie said.

Bella looked at the long line, filled not just with New Orleans residents, but Hurricane victims from all over the gulf. "You're right, this line is getting ridiculous."

"Well, I can't stand in one place for no long amount of time," Belinda said.

"Me either," Lola agreed. "My legs can't handle it."

"It's settled then. We'll go and check on Sally, and the rest of y'all can stand in the line and get the provisions." Pearl said. She eyed Bella's ankle. "Rosemary, don't ya think you ought to have the people take a look at that leg?"

"No ma'am, it's just a sprang. They can't really do anything for it no way."

Bella, Jabari, Maggie, and the twins made their way to the back of the line. Large flat screened TVs lined the walls throughout the Astrodome. Live media footage of Hurricane Katrina played all around them. Currently they were showing footage of New Orleans residents in the downtown area, looting. A few people were getting pampers and milk for their babies. But the majority of the footage was of people stealing non-essentials, like tennis shoes and flat screen TVs.

Maggie sighed. "In a time like this, why they got to show the few ignorant folks to the world?"

Bella shook her head in agreement. "I don't know, but I sure am glad we got out when we did."

Just then, a local news reporter's voice broke in. "We're going to cut away from the footage to bring you a special report from a local celebrity, former Houston basketball star, Joshua Keys. We'll be going live to the press conference being held at the corporate office of his company Home Court Advantage in just a few moments."

"Did that man just say, Joshua Keys?" Maggie whispered to Bella. Bella shook her head, speechless. Her heart began to palpitate at the thought of being moments away from seeing Joshua's face.

"This is really going to be interesting to hear what he has to say. Ted, did you manage to get a copy of Mr. Keys speech?"

"No, but sources close to him say he's looking for his estranged wife and son."

"Yeah, Dad!" Jarbari shouted.

"Jabari, shush." Bella whispered.

"Apparently, they were living in New Orleans when the storm hit. Joshua Keys has had a love- hate relationship with the media for many years. I say love-hate, because the media loves him, but he passionately dislikes the media for what he has called over the years, its 'unfair depiction' of him. He even at one time faulted the media for the problems he experienced in his marriage."

"I for one still remember the day he announced his retirement from professional basketball. The city of Houston mourned. I will remember that day always, as the day that grown men all over Texas cried."

"Gentlemen, I don't think that's the focus here today," a female voice, Ke-Ke Jackson's, cut in.

You, tell em, girl, Bella thought. Bella always liked looking at her when she lived in Houston. She was such a thoughtful, intelligent sister.

"This is a disaster that has racked everyone, regardless of socio-economic status or class. I don't think Mr. Keys is thinking about his career right now. I think his main priority is going to be the safe return of his family. This is one of the most catastrophic disasters in our lifetime, it will be written about in history books. No one is immune. That's what Joshua Keys is going to be focused on today, and frankly, guys, that's what we should be focused on too."

"Ok, Ke-Ke, we're going to have to cut away from you," Ted said.

"Yeah, Ke-Ke, cause you making just a little too much sense, sister girl," Maggie muttered.

"It looks like Joshua Keys is taking the podium now," the announcer said.

Joshua walked up to the microphone, and for Bella, all other sounds in the crowded stadium faded away. She took in his camel colored sports coat, crisp white shirt, opened casually at the collar. He looked like he hadn't had much sleep, but God, he was beautiful. The company logo of Home Court Advantage was behind him on the wall in large gold embossed lettering. From the size of the conference room where the press conference was being held, it looked as if Joshua had done very well for himself with the company he and Mike had founded after his retirement from pro-ball. Michael stood behind Joshua. "Look, Mom, Uncle Mike!" All Bella could do was nod. Joshua adjusted the microphone.

"My wife, Bella Rose Keys and my son, Jabari Keys were living in the New Orleans Lower Ninth Ward area when the storm hit." Joshua held up a recent picture of Bella, and Jabari. "Those of you from New Orleans might know them as Rosemary and Matthew LeBlanc." Everyone in the Astrodome seemed to stop talking at once. "I am offering a one million dollar reward to anyone with information that will lead to their safe return. To my wife and my son, if you are still in New Orleans, I want to say to you, just hang on. Be tough. Don't quit."

Joshua's voice started to quiver. He lowered his head. He was quiet for a moment as he composed himself. When Joshua looked up again he was staring directly into the camera. "I love you. Hang in there. I will come for you, Bella, my beautiful Rose. I will come for you, and I will find you, baby, just like I always do. I promise." With that, Joshua turned quickly and walked away from the podium.

Mike stepped forward. "I'll take any questions, related to anything Mr. Keys just said."

"Why was Mrs. Keys living in New Orleans?"

"Any questions, related to what Mr. Keys just said," Mike repeated again.

The commentator's voice cut in over Mike's, "There you have it folks, a touching plea, from Houston's brightest star, Joshua Keys. We have never, ever, seen this side of Joshua Keys before. He is offering a generous reward for anyone with any information leading to the safe return of his wife and his son."

"Yes," Ke-Ke said, "the telephone number should be appearing on our screen now."

"Mom, Mom?" Jabari pulled on Bella's sleeve. She was in a state of shock.

"Earth to Rosemary, or Bella, or whoever you are," Maggie said, waving her hand in front of Bella's face.

Bella snapped out of her trance. "Sorry."

"Mom, I'ma find Marcus, so I can call Dad now, okay?" Bella nodded her head slowly, still stung by the words she'd just heard.

Maggie looked around at all the people pointing at them, and pulling out cell phones, wildly dialing the number up on the screen. "I don't think you need to do that. Something tells me Joshua Keys is gonna be here real soon."

CHAPTER 37

Joshua walked away from the camera to compose himself. He'd had a peace in his spirit ever since he'd prayed with his church family, but the thought of Bella and Jabari fighting for their lives in New Orleans still brought tears to his eyes. He had withheld love from Bella after she'd gotten pregnant with Jabari, and of course, he knew now that's why she'd left. But if God allowed him to find her this time, he promised himself, he'd never withhold the love he had in his heart from her again. Mike walked up to him and put a hand on his shoulder. "You did good, man, real good."

Mother Berry ran into the conference room. "Joshua, the phones have been lighting up since you got off the air. Bella and Jabari were spotted at the Astrodome!"

❧

"Boss, you gotta take a look at this!" The camera operator enlarged the photo of the last two passengers exiting the school bus.

"At this very moment, Joshua Keys is making a passionate plea for the safe return of his family, and his family is at the Astrodome. They escaped New Orleans with the Anderson kid."

"Are you sure that's them?"

"I'm sending over the photo right now."

"Well what are you waiting for? Tell Connie to wrap the Anderson story, and get over there and scoop the family reunion piece, before the other networks do. Joshua Keys is a national figure, let's do this big, and let's do it live. "

CHAPTER 38

Mike stood in front of the fireplace in his office. Assembled before him were key players from Home Court Advantage. Stan his head accountant, Carol their lead designer, Phil the facilities director, and of course his personal secretary, Mother Berry. He had called an emergency managers meeting that morning after the press conference to discuss the Hurricane Katrina situation. "Come on, folks, the best minds in the city are sitting in front of me so don't tell me there's nothing we can do."

Stan spoke first. "Mike, we just don't have the resources to accommodate that kind of population—certainly not for any extended amount of time."

"What about short term?" Mike countered.

"Well, there is Hope House. It can sleep eight maybe nine at the most," Carol chimed in.

"Yes, Carol, but there's no sense in even bringing up Hope House because it's not finished yet." Stan looked at Phil. "Is the finish date even on the horizon?"

"My guys should have it done by Friday," Phil said.

"Friday's, not terrible. I mean it's not ideal, but it's not terrible," Carol said. "Out of all the things we have on the burner, it's certainly the closest thing we have to being done."

Stan rolled his eyes. "You said yourself it only sleeps eight."

"What's your point, Stan?"

"My point is there are thousands of people displaced as a result of this storm, Carol. Thousands. Can you even begin to imagine the millions it would cost to plug that type of leak?"

"I am so sick of your patronizing attitude, Stan."

"Yeah, well, I'm sick of your pie-in-the-sky-money-grows-on-trees attitude, Carol."

"Children, please," Mike said.

Staff meetings were often like this. Stan and Carol were like oil and water. Stan was from the show-me–the-money camp, and Carol was a card carrying member of the endless-possibilities-the-sky-is-the-limit-to-what-I-can-have camp. The designers were always feuding with the money people, who could care less about the aesthetic appeal of a project. Their only interest was in coming in or under budget. Joshua managed the creative types, and Mike's staff where the bottom line folk. The brothers were constantly running interference between their two teams. Getting them to agree on what and where to spend money was harder than getting Congress to pass a bill.

Stan shook his head. "Mike, I know you and Joshua are intent on running this company on your Christian principles. Community service is one thing, but this—financially, something like this could kill us. It would be suicide."

"How about instead of focusing on impossibilities right now, Stan, we focus on possibilities, alright? Tell me what we can do. Remember, it's not our job to fix this entire situation, but New Orleans is our nearest neighbor, and we do need to do our part. Home Court Advantage will send financial aid when the time is right, but what I want to know is what can this company provide for those residents arriving in Houston today."

"Housing wise?" Carol asked.

"Yes."

"And when you say today, do you mean today as in Monday or sometime this week?" Phil asked.

"Today as in today. Tell me about Hope House, Phil. If we all got into our cars and went over there today, could we finish it?"

"Us, as in the people in this room?" Stan asked.

"The people in this room, the brothers working in the mailroom, the sistas making the copies, everybody. What if everybody got a hard hat today and everybody got out into the field," Mike asked.

Stan sat back for a moment and pondered this suggestion. His jaw relaxed a bit. "It could work. We could bill it as a Day of Caring. Recoup some of the expense on this project with the tax write off. Maybe even break even."

Carol rolled her eyes.

"Phil, what do you think?" Mike asked.

Phil scratched his head. "Everything's back in for the most part. It was gutted to the studs, but the floors are done, electrical finished, and the doors are hung. Plumbing's gotta be connected, but other than that, all it really needs is the final touches like paint, and of course the appliances, and if you wanted to get somebody in there right away, we'd need furniture. I'd say if we took everybody, we could have the job done in about five hours."

Mike's phone vibrated on the table. Mother Berry picked it up. "Hello, Joshua." Mike nodded to Mother Berry who put Joshua on speaker phone.

"Talk to me, bro," Mike said.

"I just got a call from Jabari. I'm picking them up at the east end of the Astrodome, hoping to avoid the press. Him and Bella, are both fine." Cheers and congratulations went up from all the people in the room. Mike smiled. Thank God. "What cha need?"

"There are nine people traveling with them. They're tired and hungry and they have no place to go. How soon can we have a place ready for them?"

"We'll have Hope House ready before the end of the day. Go get your family, man." Mike said.

Another round of shouts when up from the staff.

"Phil, get me a driver and a transport van to meet Josh over to the dome right away."

"I'm right on it, Mike," Phil said pulling out his phone and texting.

"Send a security detail too, just in case. We know how the media can get."

"Gotcha."

Lord knows his brother was already out of sorts. Joshua hadn't had a physical altercation in years, but if somebody stood in the way of him getting to his family right now, Mike didn't want to think about what could happen.

"Transport vehicle's on the way," Phil said looking up from his phone. Security detail too. They should meet Joshua there.

"Good. Carol, today you and your team get to do what you do best. I need you to outfit Hope House with everything you think our guests will possibly need to feel right at home."

"Try not to bankrupt us on this one, Carol."

"You know what, Stan? Talk to the hand."

"Oooh, somebody's been hanging out with the sistas at the water cooler."

"What about food and personal effects?" Carol said, ignoring Stan.

"The secretaries can handle that," Mother Berry said. "We'll stock the kitchen and make sure a meal is available when they arrive."

"Thank you, Mother Berry. That would be a huge help. Phil, I'm gonna need a truck to transport furniture, you think you can spare a man?" Carol asked.

"I'm sending my guy Galvin a heads up now. I'm also sending his contact number to your phone. He'll get you whatever you need."

"Alright, everybody assemble your teams, get your hard hats on, and meet me at the site within the hour," Mike said.

CHAPTER 39

Don't lose that kid!" Jabari was running. Well, not actually running, it was more like a power walk, in over drive. He couldn't believe it, grown men with cameras and microphones were actually chasing him. If he turned a corner, they turned the corner. If he moved towards the main entrance, they moved towards the main entrance. He'd made this trek to the front of the building five times now. They weren't even trying to hide the fact that they were following him. His dad had instructed him to meet him at the back door, in order to avoid the press. But the press had found him; now Jabari was moving quickly through the Astrodome making continual nonsensical loops trying, to no avail, to shake them. This was insane. He had to get to the east entrance. His dad would surely be there by now. And although Jabari knew his dad would never leave without him, he wasn't trying to delay this family reunion thing too much longer. For the twelfth time, Jabari rounded the bend to the corridor leading to the east entrance. This time he decided to make a run for it. "Don't lose that kid!" He heard someone call at his back. His only hope was to outrun them.

❧

Bella saw the throng of reporters chasing her son and her mother instinct kicked in. She moved as fast as her swollen ankle would allow her. "Jabari!" she screamed.

"Mom!" he called back. More reporters seemed to be coming out of the woodwork. They were swarming around her like a nest of wasps. Blood sucking wasps is what Bella thought. *Just leave us alone! Please!* Bella screamed, but just like always, the media stole her voice.

"Mrs. Keys! Mrs Keys! Is it true that you've made contact with your husband?"

"Is he meeting you here?"

"Please, just leave us alone!" she spoke this time aloud, but her voice was lost in the buzzing sea of wasps.

❧

The swarm of reporters spotted Joshua as soon as he walked into the Astrodome.

"Mr. Keys! Mr. Keys, can we get a comment!"

Joshua quickly disappeared out the door he'd come through. The swarm of reporters ran behind Joshua and were met and detained by Home Court Advantage's security detail. Moments later, Joshua reentered the Astrodome through a side door.

"Dad!" Jabari screamed.

The swarm of reporters pursuing Jabari stopped dead in their tracks. "Where?!"

Jabari ran to Joshua. Joshua scooped Jabari up into his arms and hugged him tightly. "Oh, thank God! Thank God!" Joshua said, as an ocean of cameras began flashing feverishly.

"Sorry, Dad. I tried to shake them, but they were relentless."

Joshua held Jabari tightly. Finally he released him and looked down at him. "Where are the others?"

"Mom's over there," Jabari said, pointing in Bella's direction. "Everybody else is outside waiting for you."

"There's a van and a driver outside. Take the others and go. Your mom and I will be right behind you in my truck."

Jabari nodded.

"Alright, go!" Joshua opened the door, and sent Jabari out the side door away from the reporters. A reporter approached Joshua from the pack.

"I'm from WKTV, can I get an exclusive with Jabari?" The reporter took one look at the menacing expression on Joshua's face and backed away. "I guess not."

Joshua spotted Bella in the sea of reporters. The crowd of reporters that had moments ago threatened to engulf her, completely parted and allowed Joshua room to walk through to her.

"Joshua, what's it like to be reunited with your wife and your son after so long?" a reporter called out.

"Mrs. Keys will the two of you reconcile?"

"Joshua, now that you have your family back, will you consider returning to professional ball?"

"No comment," Joshua said, never once taking his eyes off of Bella. Finally he was standing directly in front of her. He looked down at her, enfolded her in his arms, and closed his eyes. Softly Joshua kissed the crown of her head. He rocked her in his arms as the cameras rolled and the world looked on. Finally Joshua pulled away and looked into Bella's eyes. "Remember the drill?"

Bella nodded her head slightly, almost imperceptibly, though people would play the clip over and over again on YouTube in the coming months to see if she actually had. She wrapped her arms around his neck and Joshua hoisted Bella up into his arms. A camera flashed directly into Bella's face.

"Ciao, Bella," a reporter said. Joshua shot a warning look in the man's direction.

"Sorry bout that," Joshua muttered. "Comes with the territory." Bella buried her head in the nape of Joshua's neck. And for the second time that day she watched the red sea part as he carried her out of the building.

CHAPTER 40

When the transport van carrying the former Dunbar Street residents arrived at Safe Harbor, they were greeted by a large colorful banner that read, Welcome Home, New Orleans. There were smells of succulent meat roasting on several old fashioned barrel grills, and a dedicated staff of about 240 or so Home Court Advantage employees, hard at work putting the finishing touches on what would be—at least for the time being—their new home. The weary travelers all realized their hunger at the same time. Jabari, who sat in the very back, kept a visual on the black truck with his father and mother in it the whole time. As Joshua had promised, it was directly behind them. Jabari inhaled deeply. "That smells like . . . barbecue," he and Marcus both said. The two boys grinned at each other. "It sure does smell good," Pearl added.

"Pearl, you ain't never lied. I didn't know I was hungry till I got a whiff of that food," Walter said.

Thanks to the deceased man's cell phone, the tribe had been able to reach their fearless leader. The van driver picked Walter up about ten blocks away from the Astrodome.

When they pulled up in front of Hope House, the Home Court Advantage secretaries quickly surrounded the van, clucking around the weary travelers like a gaggle of mother hens.

"I'm Vernice," the leader of the group declared, "but everybody around here calls me, Mother Berry."

After a round of polite introductions, Mother Berry ushered the tribe over to a waiting picnic table laden with food. "After you eat, Devin is going to drive you over to the health clinic so you can be checked out by, Monica, our community nurse. After that, Devin will drive you back to Hope House. By then, Phil has promised me that the showers will be up and running."

"But we don't have anything else to wear. All we have is the clothes on our backs," Lola declared.

"We've already sent someone out to do some shopping for you. There's also some gift cards in your rooms when you get settled in a few days you can get over to the mall and pick out a few more things for yourselves."

"But how do you know what sizes to buy?" Lola asked.

"We're secretaries, dear, we've been buying clothes and everything else for our bosses for years. I'm a pretty good judge of size." Bella walked over and took a seat by Jabari at the picnic table. "Bella, I'd say on a good day, you're about a size 6. Maggie about an eight."

"Okay, Vernice, I believe you, don't you dare go telling my size," Lola said.

Everyone laughed.

"What I want to know is when do we get to work?" Walter said, looking around at the men hauling things in and out of the building.

"That's right," Maggie chimed in. "We aren't strangers to hard work. We appreciate what you all are doing for us, but we'd like to earn our keep, if we can."

Mike appeared beside Mother Berry. "You got my family out of New Orleans alive, as far as I'm concerned, you've already earned your keep."

"Uncle Mike!" Jabari jumped up from the table and ran into his uncle's arms. Mike lifted Jabari up off the ground and gave him a big bear hug. "Hey buddy! I sure did miss you!" Mike lowered Jabari to the ground. He touched Bella on the shoulder. "Good to see you, Bella. Josh told me you hurt your ankle."

"It's nothing really, just a sprang."

"May I?" Bella nodded and Mike stooped down and examined her ankle. The large purple bruise stood out on top of her butter colored skin. Mike frowned. Bella blushed somewhat puzzled by the kindness in his eyes.

"It looks worse than it feels, honest."

"Still, better have Monica take a look at that," Mike said.

"Devin's going to take everyone over to the health office after they finish eating," Mother Berry said.

Mike rose and extended his hand to Walter, then Maggie, and the others around the table, and another round of introductions began.

❧

"So Devin, what exactly is this place?" Walter sat in the front seat, as the van drove through the compound. The van rolled past the security station and the two large metal gates they had entered when they first arrival.

"This is Safe Harbor. It's what we in the business call an urban renewal project, a gated community in a historically low-income area."

"Never thought in a million years I'd be living in a gated community," Walter muttered.

"Well, just a few years ago all of this was what you would call a depressed neighborhood."

Belinda rolled her eyes. "Depressed like what? All the people who live here are sad?"

"No, depressed as in poor. This neighborhood was riddled with drugs and crime, many of the structures where crumbling. Some of the buildings were even condemned before Home Court Advantage brought the place. Our team of designers came in and gutted the condemned places and breathed new life into the old structures that could be saved. It really is quite an extraordinary process. When you get settled, you should go check out the before and after photos. They're hanging on the wall in the community center."

"You have a community center here?" Maggie asked.

"Yes, there's also a senior center, a social workers office, a daycare facility, and of course the public health office where we are going to right now."

"Is there a basketball court at the community center?"

Devin smiled into the rear view mirror at Marcus. "The owners are retired professional ball players, what do you think?"

Marcus grinned. "I think there is."

"Then you'd be right. Full regulation size. In fact there are a total of seven different basketball courts throughout Safe Harbor, including the ones on the playgrounds. Kind of a dream if you like basketball, but if you're into soccer like me, well, then you're kind of out of luck. What do you guys like?"

"Basketball," Marcus said.

"Fo sure," Jabari gushed.

"Yeah, most of the kids whose parents apply to live here do because their children have dreams of one day going to the NBA. I mean, who wouldn't want to be surrounded by so many legends."

Walter glanced over at Devin. "Legends?"

"NBA stars aren't a novelty around here. Kobe, Shaq, they come by from time to time. They speak at the camps and youth night, and just generally make sure the kids don't get into trouble."

"Devin, did I hear you say that people have to apply to live here? Is the process very different from any other rental process?" Maggie asked.

"Oh yes, ma'am, very. For one thing, you have to come in with three letters of recommendation. It's a very rigorous process. If an applicant has a history of drug or alcohol abuse, they have to submit to monthly drug testing and counseling."

"I don't see why anyone would put up with that," Belinda huffed.

"People do it because there's no other program like Home Court Advantage. We help people move from dependence to independence. People come here because they want a better life. They want their children to go to decent schools and have decent housing. And they want to work their way up to home ownership."

Belinda sucked her teeth. "So basically, this is section eight housing."

"No ma'am, this program is nothing like section eight. If your application is accepted and you are granted an apartment, you receive free rent for one year. During which time you visit with a financial planner who helps you work out a plan to pay your bills, save some money, get your credit score back up, and get out of debt."

"Yeah, but they get to live here for free right," Belinda said, cutting Devin off.

"No, ma'am, everyone you see here works. Even the retired elders in this community work. Everyone from the security detail at the gate, to the Home Health nurse is a volunteer who lives in this community. There are some paid staffers, but for the most part, this place is run solely by the residents." Devin pulled up in front of the Public Health office. "Houston area doctors come in and do rounds at the clinic three days a week, but for the most part it's just Nurse Monica and her assistant, Jill."

The former Dunbar Street crew walked into the clinic and was immediately greeted by Jill.

"Hello there, you must be the new Hope House residents. Welcome to Safe Harbor, and welcome to Texas. Nurse Monica has been expecting you. I'm gonna need each of you to fill out this medical history form. Then she'll call you back one at a time." Jill looked down at Walter's dried bloody leg. "She'll wanna see the ones with the most obvious injuries first."

Twenty minutes later Walter was patched up and ready to go. Nurse Monica had declared his injury to be, exactly what he had been telling everyone—just a flesh wound that would heal even if he didn't get stitches. Walter had Devin drive him back to Hope House and he got to work immediately helping the other men. Nurse Monica even made some calls about Ms. Sally who hadn't come with them to Hope House because she had been taken directly from the Astrodome to a nearby hospital. The group was all grateful to hear that Ms. Sally was stabilized and resting well, and would be able to be released into Nurse Monica's care within a day or two. Bella got ice, Tylenol, and a bandage for her ankle. Everyone else was given a clean bill of health, everyone that is, except Belinda. Nurse Monica leveled her gaze on the woman in front of her. "My professional opinion is that you need hospitalization."

"Why?" Belinda huffed. "Ain't nothing wrong with me?"

"Your heart rate is low, you're dangerously underweight, and those dark circles on your arm tell me you're a user. I bet if I had you pee in a cup, I'd find drugs in your system right now."

Belinda looked away.

"I can recommend some really good treatment programs."

"I ain't interested."

"Belinda, there are rules here. In order to remain in Safe Harbor, you must agree to some type of treatment and counseling."

"That's alright, I won't be here that long." And with that, Belinda got up and stalked out of the clinic.

CHAPTER 41

In no time at all, Hope House was complete. It was set up and decorated beautifully. The kitchen cabinets where stocked with food, and each new resident was given a week's worth of clothes. Bella helped Maggie bathe the girls and put them down to bed. Bella and Maggie where sitting outside at one of the tables sewing pillows and talking to Mike and Mother Berry when Bella looked up and saw Joshua approaching. He had disappeared shortly after he dropped Bella off at Safe Harbor. She had wondered where he'd gone, but hadn't had the guts to ask. She certainly didn't feel like she had the right. Joshua smiled at her the same way he did when he'd seen her in the Astrodome that morning. Bella blushed and looked away. She still couldn't believe or understand the grace she saw in his eyes. She had taken the child that he'd loved and fell off the planet for five years.

Joshua grabbed a hard hat off the table and slapped his hands together. "What you need me to do?"

"You can work the grills," Mike said.

"What? Naw, man I don't wanna work no grill. I came here to do man's work!" Joshua beat his chest playfully. Bella couldn't resist a smile.

"I don't want to see you nowhere near a power tool," Mike said.

Mother Berry looked at Joshua and Mike. "Didn't you boys grow up on a ranch?"

"Yeah, and I can fix anything up in here,"

"Naw, bro, stop deluding yourself, you can't. Now a horse whisperer, yeah, I'll give him that much, but as far as tools and Josh are concerned –"

Joshua grabbed Mike and put him in a head lock. The two brothers tussled playfully.

"Bella, am I lying?" Mike called from inside his brother's head lock.

Bella looked up from her sewing job. She tried to stifle a giggle as she shook her head no. She couldn't help but remember all the times she was afraid to tell Joshua when something around the house was broken. Whenever Joshua pulled out his tools and attempted to "fix" the problem, the situation quickly went from minor repair, to major replacement. Joshua released his brother and looked at Bella with a look of feigned betrayal.

"Like I said, we need a burger flipper." Mike declared.

Mike kissed Bella on the cheek. "It's good to have you back, Bella."

"Bella, Maggie, those pillows look fantastic," Carol said, admiring their handiwork.

"How is everything coming, Carol?" Joshua asked.

"Actually, can I talk to you two for a minute?"

Joshua and Mike moved out of earshot with Carol. "What's up?"

"Everything's almost done. We have a few more finishing touches, and then we'll be ready for the big reveal. But we do have a slight problem. There is space for Mr. Trendale because of the first floor apartment that the Trendales can occupy, but Harbor House was set up as transitional housing for women. There really is no space here for Marcus."

Mike shrugged. "We made the rules. Why can't we bend them?"

"Well, for one thing we'd be setting a precedent that when it comes to things like this we're willing to look at it on a case by case analysis. It's a headache I don't think any of us want to deal with. Besides, there's really no space here. I mean, he'd have to share a room with his mother."

"Aw naw, we can't play the brother like that," Joshua said.

"Especially after everything he's done," Mike said. "I tell you what, Carol, you and your team finish up. Let me talk to Marcus and his folks. I think I may have an idea."

Twenty minutes later, Carol and her team pulled everybody in for the big reveal. After all the ooohs and ahs, the former Dunbar Street residents, now new Hope House residents got ready to settle themselves into their respective rooms. Maggie, Walter, and their girls would take the two bedroom apartment on the main floor. Lola and Sally, when Sally was released from the hospital, would share a bedroom and shower on the second floor, and Belinda and Pearl would share a bedroom and a shower also on the second floor.

Bella looked around the room anxiously. She was happy for her friends, really she was, especially for Maggie, who had cried during the reveal, but she was also tired and eager to find out about her own living situation. She spotted Joshua in the dining room, deep in conversation with a young white woman. Bella backed away, determined not to interrupt. But Joshua seemed to feel her presence in the room. He turned and shot a questioning look her way. To which Bella mouthed the words: it can wait.

Joshua reached out his hand and beckoned Bella over. "Gabby, have you meet my wife, Bella? Bella this is Gabby, Gabby is a member of our marketing squad."

"Hello, Gabby," Bella said.

"So nice to finally meet you, Mrs. Keys," Gabby said, pumping Bella's arm vigorously. "I have to tell you, your husband is the best boss ever."

Bella smiled up at Joshua. "I can believe that." The three of them stood there awkwardly for a moment. "I didn't want to interrupt," Bella said.

"No please, I'm the one who's interrupting your family reunion. Josh, I'll put all of it in an email. I just want to say to you both that today has been absolutely incredible. Days like this one make me glad I came to work here."

"Thanks, Gabby," Joshua said. Gabby squeezed Bella's arm as she walked away.

Joshua smiled down at her. "What can I do for you, Bella Rose?"

"I was just wondering where Jabari and I would be staying tonight. It's just that everybody else has gotten their room assignments and . . ." Bella looked away so as not to be burned by the heat of his gaze.

"The two of you will come home tonight, with me." Joshua lowered his tall frame so that he was looking directly into her eyes. "Is that all right with you?" Bella glanced over at Jabari laughing and talking with Devin. He'd never once asked about sleeping arrangements. He just assumed they'd be going home with his daddy. "I don't think Jabari would have it any other way."

"Good, neither would I. Why don't you say goodbye to your friends, we have quite a drive ahead of us."

❧

"Here's the deal," Mike was saying to Pearl and Marcus, "there is really no room in Hope House for Marcus. So I was thinking that Marcus, you—and your family, of course, could come stay with me. I'm a bachelor, and it's not like I don't have plenty of space."

"Yo, seriously!" Marcus said.

Mike grinned. "Seriously."

"Grandma, can we?"

"Aw, yeah!" Belinda slapped Marcus a high five and started doing the running man.

"No." Pearl said.

"What?" Belinda stopped dead in her tracks. "Wait a minute, did she just say no?"

"Marcus, you go with, Mr. Dutton. Belinda and I will stay here at Hope House."

"What, how you gon speak for me?" Belinda said.

"You sure about that, Ms. Pearl? I have plenty of room."

"Mr. Dutton, my daughter is an addict. The last thing I want is for her to go embarrassing Marcus and me by stealing from you. Like I said, Belinda and I will stay here." Belinda glared at her mother and stomped off. "Marcus, give me a moment to speak with Mr. Dutton alone please."

"Sure," Marcus said. He sauntered off to the kitchen. Mike motioned for her to take a seat on the couch.

"Mr. Dutton."

"Please call me, Mike."

"Alright, then I'll have to insist that you call me, Grandma Pearl."

"Are you sure about this, Grandma Pearl? I want you to feel comfortable with this. After all, I do realize that you don't know me from Adam."

"I don't know you, but then again, I do. I know you by your actions. So far your actions show me that you're a man of God."

"Well, I am a Christian but—"

"You running from the call ain't you?" Pearl stared at Mike like she was looking into his soul.

"No ma'am, my brother's the called one, not me." Pearl chuckled and patted Mike's knee.

"Won't be long 'fore he catches you. Mike, this can't be nothing but God. My Marcus is probably your biggest fan. Ever since he was a little boy, he's wanted to play in the NBA, and be just like you. He probably had a million and one posters of you, from your ball playing days, until his mama sold them off, one by one, trying to get money for them drugs. So if you'd let Marcus stay at your place for a while, it would mean a lot to him and me." Mike wrapped the older woman in his arms.

"Grandma Pearl, it would be my great honor.

CHAPTER 42

Joshua, Bella, and Jabari said their goodbyes, and made their trek out of the city. By the time they arrived home Jabari was sound asleep. Joshua tried rousing him a couple of times to no avail.

"I should warn you he's nearly impossible to awake when he's this tired." Bella said.

"Wait right here," Joshua walked around to the back seat, lifted Jabari up and carried him into the house. Five minutes later he came back out to the garage and opened Bella's car door. "That boy has gotten a lot bigger and a lot heavier since the last time I carried him up those stairs."

"I know. Sometimes I look at him, and I can't believe he's the same little peanut we brought home from the hospital."

"How's your ankle?"

"Better now since I took the Tylenol. You don't have to carry me, Josh. Really, I can walk."

Josh turned on the overhead light, and inspected Bella's foot. When he touched her Bella drew back. Not from pain, as he had suspected, but from the spark of electricity that spread throughout her body at his touch.

"Liar, grab my neck." Bella reached her arms out and encircled Joshua's neck. He scooped her up and Bella felt her stomach do a backwards flip. She took in the scent of his familiar aftershave and buried her face into his neck. Five years, and he still smelled the same. Joshua climbed the stairs to the upstairs bedrooms.

"I'm gonna put you in our old room for tonight. We'll work out the details of more permanent sleeping arrangements in the morning. I'll be down the hall in the guest room if you need anything."

It was amazing, she thought, how much she missed being in his arms without really knowing all along that this was exactly what she missed. She hoped that he couldn't feel her heart beating a mile a minute. But of course he could.

"Why are you afraid?" Joshua asked.

"Hum?"

"I felt your heart racing like this at the Astrodome. At first I thought it was the crowds, now I'm beginning to think that you're afraid I'll drop you."

She raised her head and looked into his eyes.

"I mean I'm not in the gym everyday anymore, but I'm still pretty fit."

She laughed.

"I'd never drop you, Bella."

"I know that."

"Then why is your heart about to beat out of your chest?"

"Believe me, it's not for the reasons you think." *Oh, God I can't believe I said that out loud.* Her face colored with embarrassment.

Joshua smiled and set her down gingerly on the carpeted floor in the master bedroom.

Bella looked around the large master suite. "Wow, everything looks exactly the same as when I left. Except this." Bella pointed to the 42 inch flat screen TV that now flanked the north wall of the room.

"Weren't you the one who always said televisions don't belong in here?" Once the words were out, Bella regretted them immediately. She saw the shadow of pain pass across Joshua's eyes. "Joshua, I'm —I shouldn't have said that."

"It's cool. I changed the sheets this afternoon. I just need to get some towels out the dryer. I know you showered at Hope House, but I figured you'd want to take another one in the morning."

Bella nodded.

"I tried to get things as neat as possible, the maid doesn't come again till Friday." So that's where he had disappeared to this afternoon. He was at home cleaning.

"Everything looks great, really. You did a wonderful job, Josh. Thank you."

He nodded. "I'll get those towels." He turned on his heels and was gone.

Bella walked into their master closet and saw her clothes hung by color and season just the way she had left them. All her shoes lined up by style and occasion, just the way she had left them. Her brushes, combs, lotions, and crèmes were all exactly where she had left them. He hadn't changed a thing. Bella began to cry, deep, heavy, body quaking sobs. She cried for her life and for the choices she'd made. When Joshua returned, he founded her sitting on the large ottoman that flanked her closet floor sobbing her eyes out. Joshua dropped the towels and knelt beside her. He folded her into his arm and held her till her sobs quieted.

"What's the matter, Bella? Is anything hurting you?"

She shook her head.

"Then why are you crying?"

"It's just that everything's the same, but different."

"What's different now?"

"I don't know. I just feel so much love here."

Joshua pulled her tighter and kissed the top of her head. "Oh, baby. I wish I could take credit for that, but I can't. That's the presence of God you feel here, Bella. This closet has been my prayer chamber since the day you left me." He pointed to a Bible on a pillow in the corner of the room. "I've been known to do my fair share of weeping in here, where no one can hear me but the Big Man Himself." Bella looked at him quizzically, but she wasn't ready to ask questions, not just yet.

The silence hung in the air between them, until Joshua asked another question. "Is that why you left me because you didn't feel loved?"

Bella shook her head. "I was foolish, Joshua. You loved Jabari. That should have been more than enough for me."

"But it wasn't, so what else did you need that I wasn't giving you?"

She shook her head. "It doesn't matter now." Bella grabbed a tissue off her vanity table and blew her nose. Joshua rose, went to the bathroom and returned with a warm face towel. Gently he wiped her tear streaked face. "Tell me."

"It doesn't matter, and, it won't change anything."

"Maybe, but then again, it may change everything."

"I guess what I needed most was for you to stay for the right reasons. After I got pregnant, you stayed, because I needed you and I should have been grateful for that. I had no right to deserve anything more, but I needed you to need me."

Joshua's eyes peered down at her. "So it was a question of desire then. You left because you didn't think I desired you?" Never breaking eye contact with her, Joshua unbuttoned his shirt, he pulled her hand to him and pressed it up against to his hard, warm, chest. Bella felt the strong, quick, rhythm of his heart. Lord. Have. Mercy. Had he not been holding on to her wrist so tightly, Bella surely would have passed out.

"All this time, you never knew that my heart races for you? That my palms get sweaty, that my tongue sticks to the roof of my mouth whenever I'm near you?" Joshua dropped her hand then. "I don't believe that, Bella. Not for a moment. Our problems were never in the bedroom. It was in all the other rooms of the house that we had our trouble. So tell me the truth." He lifted her chin and saw a new puddle of tears forming in her eyes. This time instead of wiping them away with the towel, he kissed them slowly, one by one. "Why'd you leave me, baby, huh." His voice was raspy.

"I left so that I could become someone you could love, someone who was worth it."

"I loved you so much, Bella Rose. I still love you." His lips found her mouth then and he filled hers with a powerful kiss.

CHAPTER 43

Mike's hand reached for the vibrating phone on the bedside table in the darkened room. "Hello."

"Mikey, this is your father. Open the door, we're outside." Mike sat up in bed and planted his feet on the cold floor. He rubbed his hand over his balled head and cradled the phone to his ear with his shoulder "You're kidding, right?"

"Yeah, but it would serve you right if I wasn't. We try and respect you boys' privacy and this is how you repay us."

"Dad, look, I swear I told Josh to call you guys."

"Can you tell me why we had to watch our own grandson's homecoming on YouTube? Ted from the General calling, asking all kinds of questions that I should know the answers to, and I'm sitting here blubbering like some dag gone idiot, because I don't know what the heck is going on!"

"Yeah, sorry about that."

"You boys hold a national press conference and tell the world that Jabari and Bella were living in New Orleans at the time of the flood! And you can't even make one simple phone call home to your mother! She had to watch the whole thing on CNN!"

"I should have had someone call you."

"Darn right you should have!"

Mike could hear his mother's voice in the background. "Tell Mikey we're on our way. I'll meet you in the car, Jack."

"You hear that, Mikey? Your mother's on her way to the car." Jack let out a string of expletives once his wife was out of earshot. "See what you've done," now I've got to put on pants, when here I've been naked now for a whole week!"

Mike groaned. "No, don't! Don't get in the car."

"Got to drive all the way out there cause you boys act like you don't have the good sense God gave ya! You know I hate coming to the city!"

"Yes, I know. Do me a favor, stay home, Dad, please. I'm begging you. Put Mom on the phone."

"What?"

"I said put Mom on the phone!"

"Oh, okay, hold on a minute. Mel, Mikey wants to talk to you!"

Melissa picked up the phone. "Mikey, are you boys okay? How's Bella and Jabari? I've been trying to call your brother all morning. He's not answering his phone."

"Mom, listen, I'm really sorry I didn't get to you guys sooner, but everyone's fine. I don't want you and Dad on the road, okay? We still have a lot of Hurricane Katrina folks coming into the city. The traffic is backed up for days. I'm sure Josh and Bella are just exhausted, and seeing that it isn't even six AM yet I'm pretty sure they're still sleeping. I'm on my way over there later on this morning."

"What time?"

"Later, when the sun comes up. You'll talk to everyone before the end of the day. I promise, okay? I'll call you from Josh's."

"Alright, Mikey, I love you."

"Love you too. Bye."

CHAPTER 44

Joshua awoke to Houston sunlight filtering through the Texas sky. He inhaled the scent of Bella's naturally curly hair sprayed across his pillow. Their bodies had become so naturally one last night, he couldn't tell where his limbs ended and hers began. *Man, what ever happened to taking things slow?* He knew he had just complicated their already complicated situation. And the messed–up thing about it was that this was nowhere near what Joshua had intended. He had planned on getting her settled into the master bedroom and then taking up residence in the guest room down the hall. But she'd been so beautiful and so vulnerable last night. And the things she had said about him not wanting her, not needing her, it made him want to express all the love he had in his heart for her. *God, what have I done? You know this woman hasn't been faithful to me, for all I know she could have a sexually transmitted disease.* His plea to the Father gave him no relief. In fact, staring down at her like this, all he wanted to do was make love to her again and again, make up for lost time. All the words of affirmation he should have spoken to her but didn't because of the pain that was in his heart. He could say those things now. Joshua reached around under the sheet, he slipped his boxers on, and got up out of the bed. The one good thing about all of this was that Jabari didn't know anything about it, and if things didn't work out between him and Bell—

"Pssh, Dad?"

Joshua looked up to see Jabari standing in the doorway. Joshua eyes flew immediately back over to the bed. "Uh . . . hey, son, what's up?"

Jabari seemed as tickled as a kid on Christmas day to find his parents in bed together. This should be natural not . . . *awkward.*

"I don't have any clothes," Jabari whispered in a barely audible voice.

Of course he didn't. The clothes in Jabari's closet were all five years too small. He couldn't wear any of them. Joshua walked into to the large master closet with Jabari following behind him. "You can wear something of mine, just until we get over to the store today and do some shopping for you." Joshua removed a pair of shorts with an elastic waist band, and an NBA t-shirt from his closet drawer.

"Thanks, Dad."

"Jabari, why are you whispering?"

"I don't want to wake up Mom. This is the first time she hasn't woke up with a nightmare in like, I don't know, forever." Jabari tiptoed out of the bedroom. A minute later, Joshua heard Jabari's bedroom door close.

Joshua stood in doorway staring at Bella's resting form. So the nightmares were back. When he first married Bella she had horrible dreams. She hated when he was on the road because she said whenever he left, the nightmares always returned. As a young husband he didn't have the understanding that he had now. He didn't know that he was his wife's covering. That he could bless her and anoint her, and pray over her dream world. This is exactly what he did now. Joshua walked over to her and knelt at the side of the bed. While Bella slept, he prayed.

Bella awoke to find Joshua sitting beside her on the edge of the bed. He curled a tendril of her hair around his finger.

"What were you doing just now?" she asked.

"Praying for you."

"You really have changed. I guess what the media is saying about you this time is true."

Joshua raised an eyebrow. "Yeah, what's that?"

"That you found religion."

Joshua chuckled softly. "Geez, I hope not."

Bella stared at him, the same puzzled look from the night before on her face.

Joshua took her hands in his. "A lot of things have changed for me, Bella. After you and Jabari left, I recommitted my life to Christ. When I lost you, He kept me from losing my mind."

"Yeah, about that, Joshua . . . I don't know how to tell you how so—"

Joshua put his finger to her lips. "The only thing I want you to tell me right now is how you feel this morning."

"I feel fine."

He turned on the bedside lamp and examined her face in the light. "I want you to see a doctor right away."

"Nurse Monica gave me a clean bill of health, remember?"

"Yeah, I know, but you look a little green about the gills to me."

"Lately my stomach's been a little queasy in the mornings, but it usually settles down after I get a bite to eat."

"Then I'll go make breakfast, any special requests?"

Bella wrapped her arms around his neck and pulled him back down on top of her. “Does it have to be food?”

He ran his hands through her thick curly mane and placed a quick peck on her lips. “For now, yes.”

“Then no, no special request. Surprise me.”

“Surprise you, huh?”

She nodded and he kissed her slowly, tenderly, deliberately, before rising up off the bed.

“Come on down when you’re ready.”

CHAPTER 45

Joshua was in the kitchen cooking breakfast when the doorbell rang. He clicked on the television in the kitchen and turned to the security camera station. The cameras round his home allowed him to see approaching visitors from every angle of his property. Joshua saw his brother and Marcus standing outside on the front porch.

Joshua opened the front door and greeted Mike then Marcus with an easy handshake and chest bump. Mike took in Josh's appearance, his feet were bare and he was clad in a pair of boxers and a t-shirt. His brother looked happier than he had seen him in years.

"What you getting into this morning?" Mike asked.

"Just making a little breakfast, want some?"

"Naw. We gon head out and grab a bite in a minute."

"Jabari, we got company!" Joshua shouted.

Jabari came bounding down the stairs. "Hey, Uncle Mike! Hey, Marcus, what's up?"

"Hey, shorty, what up?" Marcus said.

"My man, Marcus and I are gon go shoot some hoops this morning. We stopped by to see if you wanted to tag along," Mike said.

"Cool, Dad, can I?"

"Yeah man, but first things first, we need to get you some clothes. How you gonna hoop in those?"

"That's exactly what I was explaining to this young man right here. I was hoping Marcus could sport some of your gear till we made it over to the mall today."

Joshua looked at Marcus. Mike was 6'.8" and Josh stood at 6'.6." And although it was pure muscle, Mike was also about twenty pounds heavier than Joshua. In his brother's clothes, Marcus looked as lost as Jabari did in Joshua's gear this morning. "I'll hook him up. Bella's upstairs right now, but when she comes down you can take him up to pick something out."

Mike raised an eyebrow, at the mention of Bella, but said nothing. "Cool."

"Dad, I don't think you understand, I'm a baller, every time I play, I bring my A game. So it really doesn't matter what I wear on the court. The way I see it, I might as well hoop in these."

Joshua pulled green peppers, mushrooms, and red onions, out of the refrigerator, all things he knew Bella would love in her omelet. "Jabari, please, you can bring whatever game you like. You can bring your Z game, your uncle will still crucify you."

Mike clapped his hands in agreement and let out a hoot.

"And if you gotta stop every five minutes to pull up your drawers, he really ain't gon show you no mercy," Joshua said.

Mike balled his fist up and made a gruesome face at Jabari. He spoke in a low sinister voice. "No mercy."

"Aw, Marcus, I see these old dudes got jokes."

"Josh, this kid just call us old, I'm a have to take 'em to school."

Joshua slapped Mike a high five. "Take 'em to school, bro."

Marcus lifted a hand in the air. "I just want to say, for the record, that was Jabari, not me."

Mike laughed and threw his arm around Marcus' shoulder. "Marcus, you may have noticed, that in this family talking junk and basketball go hand in hand. My nephew here has, apparently, during his tenure in New Orleans, learned the fine art of talking junk, but the real question is—"

"Can he play some ball," Joshua said.

Mike gave Joshua a fist bump.

"I can hold my own, right, Marcus?" Jabari said.

"You do alright, shorty."

"We gotta pick up some things for Marcus today. Might as well take Jabari and get some clothes for him too. That way you and Bella can hang back a bit, chill for a while."

Joshua grinned. "Thanks man, we'd appreciate that."

Bella came downstairs, wearing Joshua's robe. This picture of her in the morning was so unnatural yet at the same time completely natural, because Joshua had seen it a million times before. If it wasn't for the sensation of the cold marble tile beneath his feet, Joshua wouldn't have believed that the moment was real. His family was actually here. His wife was standing in his kitchen wearing his bath robe. She had a zillion robes in her closet, but as always, she preferred to wear his. Most days this was frustrating to Joshua, especially since Bella's petite 5'.2" frame caused several inches of his robe to drag against the floor. Today, however, it was endearing.

"Good Morning," Bella sang as she walked into the kitchen.

"Hey, mom," Jabari said kissing her cheek.

"Bella," Mike said, kissing her other cheek. "Don't you look relaxed."

Bella blushed and took a seat at the counter. Joshua sat a mug of mint tea in front of her. She lifted the mug to her lips and smiled over the rim at him with her eyes.

"Marcus, did you sleep well last night?" Bella asked.

"Yes, ma'am."

"Have you called your grandma yet?"

"Uh . . . no, ma'am, but I'm fixing to call them today though."

"Speaking of calling mamas, Josh, dad called my house this morning at 5:30 and chewed me out."

Joshua put his fist to his mouth. "Man, I totally forgot about them. You think they saw any footage?"

"The press conference on CNN, and you and Bella's little family reunion on YouTube."

"We're on YouTube?" Bella asked.

"As of this morning, it's the number one watched video in America. Mother Berry called me about an hour ago. Number two is the press conference, entitled, Joshua Keys' Passionate Pleas for his Family's Return," Mike said.

"They must be worried sick." Joshua said.

Mike shrugged. "At first, now they're just pissed."

"Jabari, quick." Joshua threw Jabari the house phone. "Call your grandparents."

Jabari fumbled but managed to catch the phone. "I don't know the number."

"Push the scroll button. It's probably the last ten numbers on the Caller ID."

"Oh, here it is," Jabari said. "It's ringing. Hey, Grandma Mel, it's me, Jabari. I'm fine. Mom's fine too. Yeah, Dad, is too. Un huh. No. Hey, Grandpa Jack, yes, I can hear you both. Everybody's standing right here. Well, me, Dad, Mom, Uncle Mike, and my friend, Marcus. He's staying with Uncle Mike for now. Huh?"

Jabari laughed. "Yeah." Jabari covered the receiver with his hand. "Grandma wants to know if Marcus is the one who hotwired the school bus."

"Wow, they really have been keeping up with the coverage," Bella said.

"Marcus, my Grandma Mel says thank you for saving our lives."

Marcus shrugged. "It's cool."

"He said you're welcome. Okay, hold on." Jabari pulled the phone away from his ear. "Dad, Grandma wants to know when we coming down."

"You better give her something man, you owe 'em big time," Mike said.

"Jabari, put your grandma on speakerphone," Joshua said. Jabari pushed the speakerphone button and set the phone down on the countertop.

"Hey Mom."

Melissa's voice filled the kitchen. "Joshie, is that you?"

"Yes, Mom, it's me."

"We're not speaking to you, young man," Jack said.

"Hey Dad, good to hear your voice too," Joshua said dryly.

"Hey Dad, my eye, where's Bella!"

"Hi, Mel. Hi, Jack. I'm right here," Bella said.

"Honey, you don't know what it means to us to hear your voice after all this time."

"It's good to hear your voice too, Mel."

"Mikey told us not to come down because you had so much traffic out your way with Hurricane victims coming into the city."

You owe me. Mike mouthed to Joshua.

"So when are you all coming this way?" Mel asked.

"Mom, how does this weekend sound? I know you're dying to see Jabari and he really wants to see you too," Joshua said.

"Why this weekend sounds wonderful, dear. Mikey, are you there?"

"Yes, ma'am."

"Will you be coming too?"

"On one condition."

"What's that, dear?"

"Dad's gotta wear pants."

Joshua looked at Mike. "I thought he was kidding about that, is he really walking around the house naked?"

"As a jay bird." Mel sighed. "Now that you boys are gone, the things I have to put up with."

"I'll make you boys a deal," Jack said.

"What's that?" Mike said.

"If Bella Rose comes, I'll put on pants."

Bella laughed.

"Bella Rose, I hope you hear that. I swear this man is absolutely incorrigible," Mel said.

"Jabari, bring the young man who stole the bus. I can't wait to meet him. He sounds like my kind of guy," Jack said.

"Okay, Grandpa, I will."

"Hey, Jabari, do me one more favor. Tell your dad to kiss your mom for me. I'd tell him to do it myself, but I'm not talking to the big lug." Joshua smiled.

"Dad, Grandpa Jack wants you to kiss mom."

"Okay, Dad," Joshua said.

"And none of that top of the head, made for TV crap we saw on YouTube. I want him to really lay it on her. Well, is he doing it, cause I'm not hanging up until he does."

"Josh, go ahead and kiss the woman, please, so we can hang up the phone," Mike said. Josh leaned into the counter and kissed Bella softly and slowly on the lips.

"Alright, he kissed her," Mike said. "Lots of love to you both, see you this weekend." And with that Mike hung up the phone. Joshua and Bella were still kissing.

"Come on guys, let's go up and get Marcus some clothes so we can break camp."

Bella pulled away then. "Mike, aren't you guys going to stay for breakfast?" she called up the stairs after them.

"We're going out to eat," Mike called back over his shoulder.

"Mike offered to take Marcus and Jabari shopping this morning so we could have some alone time. I hope that's okay with you?"

"Are you kidding me? That sounds prefect," Bella purred. Joshua set the spinach and feta omelet in front of Bella and watched her face turn one, two, no— three, shades of green.

"Excuse me," Bella took off running for the half bath down the hall. Moments later, Joshua heard the sound of her insides slapping against the toilet bowl, and he knew. He knew from the depths of his soul, that he was re-living the most horrific moment of his life. The toilet flushed, and her feet padded back into the kitchen. Bella wiped the side of her mouth clean with a paper towel. She looked up and saw Joshua staring at her. "What?"

"How far along are you?"

She shook her head, not understanding the question.

"You're pregnant, Bella."

"No, it can't be. I told you my stomach's been upset."

"It's the onions right?"

"Yes, but—"

"You love red onions, but when you were pregnant with, Jabari, you couldn't stand the sight of them."

"I'm—no. God no." Bella laid her head down on the countertop. She began counting back the days since her last cycle in her mind.

"So, how far along are you?" Joshua's voice was distant, causal, detached. The sudden gulf between them made her cry.

"Hum, I don't know, a month maybe. Early enough to still get an abortion," she said softly.

He stepped away from her, repulsed. "You don't know me at all, if you think I would ever pay for something like that."

"Josh—"

He put his hand up to stop her. "How could you do this, Bella? How could you come back to me this way, twice?"

"Please, hear me out—" Bella stopped speaking abruptly when she heard the sound of the others coming down the stairs.

"Bye Mom, bye Dad!" Jabari called from the front foyer. There was the sound of the front door opening then banging shut. Mike walked into the kitchen next. He looked at Joshua, then Bella.

"Everything alright?"

Silence.

"We bout to head out."

"Wait. I'm coming."

Mike looked at Bella, "You sure bout that, bro? Cause if you got business you need to take care of here, we can catch up later."

"Naw, man, I gotta get outta here, now." Joshua walked out the kitchen and headed upstairs to the bedroom.

"We'll be in the car," Mike called to Joshua's back. Mike lifted Bella's chin and wiped the tears from her face. "My brother loves you, Bella. Whatever it is, the two of you can work through this." Mike hugged Bella tightly before he left.

Moments later, she heard Joshua come downstairs and the front door close behind him.

CHAPTER 46

"Good game, boys," Mike said, slapping them both high fives. "Hit the showers." Mike watched Jabari and Marcus trot off towards Home Court Advantage's locker rooms. Then he turned his attention to Joshua on the other end of the court, driving the ball into the hoop like a mad man. Between Bella's tears and Joshua's brooding silence this morning Mike wasn't getting a good feeling about this. He walked down to the other end of the court. "Yo, talk to me, Josh. You've barely said ten words since we left your house this morning. What's up?"

Joshua wiped the sweat on his brow with the edge of his t-shirt. "We didn't come here to talk, remember? We came here to play ball." Joshua slammed the ball into the hoop with so much force the fiberglass backboard shook.

"What happened with you and Bella this morning, man?"

Slam! Joshua's body soared through the air as he slam dunked the ball into the hoop.

"Twenty four hours ago, you were ready to charter a plane, and comb the earth looking for the woman. This morning you leave her in your kitchen crying. What's up?"

"She's pregnant."

"So that's why you round here slapping that ball into the hoop like you crazy? This complicates things between you and Bella. But you got this. You're good at this fatherhood thing."

Joshua drove strong for the hoop and stuffed the ball into the net. He hung from the rim for a few seconds before dropping to the floor with the agility of a cat.

"Wait a minute, man. Is it even possible to know this early?"

Joshua starred at him. The smile disappeared from Mike's face as understanding sank in. "Damn. You sure?"

"I know my wife. I know her body, and least you forget, I've been through this with Bella before. Yeah, I'm sure." Joshua drove hard and mashed the ball into the hoop.

"I gotta ask you, bro. Even though I know you don't want to hear it now. What He telling you to do?"

Joshua shook his head. "It doesn't matter what I think I hear, Mike. I'm getting a divorce."

"I'm just sayin', He God, right? He know everything. Omnipotent—least that's what you always tell us. So even as bad as this is, He had to have known about it. Right?"

Joshua glared at him, and Mike knew that for the first time today he had gotten through to his brother.

Joshua drove the ball hard into the hoop one last time and headed off towards the showers.

CHAPTER 47

Bella sat in the kitchen with her head on the cold, hard, granite countertop for a long time. Joshua's words playing over and over like a tape recording in her mind. *How could you do this, Bella? How could you come back to me this way, twice?*

Ten years ago when he found out that she was pregnant with Jabari, he had asked another series of questions, one after another, in rapid succession, right after he vowed to kill the man.

"Did he rape you? Did he force you? Did he hurt you?"

"He didn't rape me. He didn't hurt me. He didn't make me. I did this, Joshua. Me, on my own." When he had finally quieted enough to really hear what she was saying, he got up and walked out of the front door. It was two o'clock the next afternoon when Joshua finally returned, and he was drunk.

"Just one more question, Bella. Why?"

She couldn't answer him. Not because she didn't want to, but because she didn't have the tools to. She couldn't explain, why being with this older man whom she didn't love and whom she knew didn't love her was safer than being with him. Why every time she looked into her husband's eyes and saw the love he had in his heart for her, why it made her feel safe, and swallowed at the same time. She couldn't tell him that his love was changing her. That it had changed her. That for her now, he was both water and air. This sensation scared her to death, so much so that she needed to do the leaving first, because if he ever left her, she would surely die. So she'd had an affair with her World History professor. Why? Because life couldn't, it shouldn't feel this good. And her experience had been that sooner or later, the bottom always dropped out of something good.

Joshua had sat there, on their living room floor staring up at her for forty minutes with blood shot eyes, waiting for her to respond. And because she couldn't say the truth, she did the only thing she thought she could do in a situation like this. It was during the time of his first paternity suit, so she lied.

"I was afraid . . . I thought if this baby turned out to be yours you'd leave me, so I decided to do the leaving first."

"I told you, I've never laid eyes on that woman in my life. Bella Rose, don't you trust me? Don't you know I'd never deceive you?" He laughed then an awful wounded laugh. "But, you can't even trust your own daddy, now can you? So how in the hell are you ever gon be able to trust me?"

Déjá vu. Their lives had come full circle. Again. All she could do was think about the question he'd asked her ten years ago, and the question he'd asked her today. "Why?"

Heaven help her, because the answer was still the same.

Author's Note

Okay, so as you can clearly see, our story isn't over. You've just read *Passing Through Water*, book 1 of the four part series entitled, *Redemption's Price*. In a nod to the old school series literature I use to love, I've decided to leave our beloved hero and shero metaphorically dangling from a bridge.

Books 1-3 of this series focus on Joshua and Bella and how the redemption plan of God plays out in their lives. Book 4 is a long-awaited spin off featuring Joshua's tall, dark and handsome older brother, Mike Dutton, AKA The Man of Steel. Mike's story is our season finale, and I can promise you that it's one you won't want to miss! Look for part two, of the Joshua and Bella saga, *Opening the Floodgates*, to be released this upcoming February, Valentine's Day weekend 2016.

In the meantime you can check us out online at www.ironerspress.com, you can read a sneak preview of *Opening the Floodgates*, as well as find out about all of the other great books, services, and products that The Ironer's Press has to offer. Until we meet again, blessings to you and your household.

Sincerely,

Catrina J. Sparkman

Discussion Questions for Book Clubs

1. Which character did you identify with the most? Explain why? Which character did you find the hardest to connect with? Explain why?

2. This story is based loosely on the Biblical story of Hosea yet the main character is named Joshua. Discuss they symbolism connected to names in this novel. Why do you think the author chose to name the main character Joshua instead of Hosea? Is there any other symbolism in the novel related to names that you see?

3. Identify and discuss themes you see in the novel.

4. What role, if any, does intercession play in getting the Dunbar Street Residents out of New Orleans?

5. Officer Timothy O'Brien tells Bella that God has decided to redeem her. He also tells Bella's father he will not stop praying until Bella is free. If God had decided to redeem Bella, as officer O'Brien suggests, why would prayer be necessary at all? What part, if any, does prayer play in God's redemption process?

Made in the USA
Lexington, KY
25 February 2017

Made in the USA
Lexington, KY
25 February 2017